D1766512

Loffing Matters

edited by
Paul McDonald

Tindal
Street
Press

First published in July 2006 by
Tindal Street Press Ltd.
217 The Custard Factory, Gibb Street, Birmingham B9 4AA
www.tindalstreet.co.uk

ISBN 0 9547913 5 5
EAN 978 0 9547913 5 3

Typeset by Country Setting, Kingsdown, Kent.
Printed and bound in Great Britain by Clays Ltd, St Ives PLC

Loffing Matters

Contents

Introduction

Why are there so few collections of humorous short stories around? I mean modern ones, without P. G. Wodehouse in? Collections of every other kind of modern short story abound. Horror, crime, science fiction, football related, drug inspired, dream inspired, dysentery inspired (aka travel inspired), postmodern, post-postmodern. But where are the humour stories? Well here, at last. It's about time, because it only takes a moment's reflection to realize how much laughing matters. Certainly it matters in fiction. Humour is fundamental to storytelling and has been from the start. There are jokes in Homer (not Homer Simpson, the other one). Admittedly he'd die on his arse at the Comedy Store, but you get the point. And there does seem to be a special relationship between humour and the short story. Think about it: Stephen Leacock, James Thurber, Dorothy Parker, Garrison Keillor, Edgar Allan Poe (maybe it's just me with the last one). Something about the short story lends itself to humour. Perhaps it has to do with brevity being the soul of wit, but this is no place to theorize; rather it's the place to celebrate the fact that we have a modern collection of comic stories at last.

It's a fact worth celebrating because laughing matters and, if you happen to come from the Black Country, so does *loffing*. But don't let the book's title mislead you. These stories are regional in that some were inspired by the area, but you won't find Anuk and Ali in these pages. What you'll find is challenging, culturally aware literary fiction that interrogates social mores with a wit and insight that should appeal to all intelligent readers.

Many of these stories have laugh-out-loud moments but writing doesn't have to be joke-laden to be funny. A subtle yet powerful humour, for instance, informs the work of John Mulcreevy. His two stories explore the regenerative potential of art. In 'Joe Stalin's Ape' a papier-mâché gorilla becomes a symbolic – and irresistibly comic – outlet for his obdurate, frustrated hero, while in 'Wicked, Deliciously So', Mulcreevy addresses the relationship between creativity and subversion. Here two pensioners strive to challenge a system that has consigned them to the scrapheap, partly via their artwork, and partly via a more direct route: shoplifting. Both stories are satires of a society that thwarts rather than facilitates creative energy. As with many of the tales in *Loffing Matters*, the clash between individuals and their meagre environment becomes a source of painful, poignant humour.

Liza Granville is the one contributor who doesn't have significant regional affiliations, but we won't hold that against her, or her gloriously malevolent tales. In 'Neapolitan Ice' she plays with cultural stereotypes, partly for the sheer fun of it, and partly to let us reflect on their implications. Her hero – a Pompeii tour guide – finds his illicit money-making scheme comically undermined in a story which links corruption, chauvinism and excess to the history of Western culture. Granville's humour is effortless and delightfully venomous, not least in 'Flower Power', a tale of a malicious young woman, Tryphena, whose rage at the world manifests itself in the most excessive forms of filial rebellion. Here she creates a merciless satire of naïve hippie consciousness, and the absurdities of conceptual art.

The stories of Birmingham-based Laurence Inman examine the narratives that govern our lives. The eponymous hero of 'Danny the Bastard' finds his trajectory determined by masculine codes of honour: his tragedy is that he adheres to these codes despite the consequences. Danny is a middle-aged gangster for whom 'time is really beginning to mean it' but he still can't resist acting like a child. 'New Departures', meanwhile, deals with a different sort of life-shaping narrative: the rat race. Though the hapless schoolteacher, Almond, is liberated from his job by the worldly-wise Lazenby, the story develops into one which cleverly questions the value or, indeed, the possibility of escape. Of course, the author offers no easy answers for his characters – what he offers are erudite, hilarious explorations of age-old dilemmas.

The narrator of Joan Michelson's story, 'To Catch a Thief', assumes she's become the butt of her own joke when a 7-Eleven manager disappears. 'Go rob a bank,' she told him, and perhaps he's followed her advice. That's the thing with jokes: they have a double meaning. It's what makes them interesting, and it's what makes Joan Michelson's fiction interesting too: it always points in more than one direction. The American-born author taught creative writing in the Black Country for many years, and the humour in her second story, 'An Ace in the Midlands', stems partly from New World perspectives on Old World eccentricities, and partly from the predicament of her narrator, Joey. In his letters home his prose dances and his talent jumps off the page. So why is he unpublished? Perhaps he's the victim of his own perfectionist impulse, which compels him to revise ad infinitum. In this respect the story is a cry for help: a reaching to a place beyond the world of writing. We might have imagined him correcting his 'uncorrected proof' for ever, were we not holding evidence to the contrary in our hands.

Paul McDonald

Life is hard for all of the protagonists in *Loffing Matters*. It's hard for superfluous pensioners, impecunious tour guides and alienated artists. Life is hard for men trapped in the tramlines of inevitability, exploited 7-Eleven workers, or tutors who rhapsodize to deaf ears. When life is hard, then laughing, and *loffing*, matters. Life is better if you can. Read these stories and see.

Paul McDonald
May 2006

John Mulcreevy

JOHN MULCREEVY's first story appeared in *Platform*, a 1970s school magazine. After school he spent time cutting things – steel sheets, grass lawns – and drawing things – cartoon strips, the dole. His short fiction has also been published in *Birmingham Noir* and *Birmingham Nouveau* (Tindal Street Press, 2002).

Wicked, Deliciously So
John Mulcreevy

On Clive's last day the staff gathered round his desk at Birmingham New Street Station with a gift-wrapped bottle of Teacher's Highland Cream and a wooden box. Whisky was spilled into glasses while Clive eased off the box's ribbon. He nodded approvingly at the message on his leaving card: 'Now you'll be able to colour in all those trains.'

He flipped up twin clasps revealing the contents of the watercolour painting set: tubes of pigment, brushes, a small palette and a bottle of masking fluid. A decent brand: he was impressed.

The assembly gulped booze then launched into 'For He's a Jolly Good Fellow'. Cheek pecks from the four women and back slaps from the four men ended the party.

'Enjoy your retirement, and how about one last announcement for the road?'

After eighteen years of informing the frustrated concourse that this train has been delayed, that train has been cancelled, has anyone mislaid a child – about five years old, duffel coat, Bart Simpson backpack – Clive's voice changed from a soft nasal burr to the indecipherable repine of a British Rail announcer for the final time.

'This'll be a first,' he said, craning his neck into the

microphone. 'The five forty-five from Liverpool Lime Street will be arriving . . . on time.'

And that was how Clive retired, his end theme a brew of laughter from his colleagues. Soon the only reminder he'd ever been there would be the *Flying Scotsman* sketched in biro on the back of a memo Blu-Tacked to the wall by his desk.

He didn't think they'd replace him; at least not with a man. In the future, the service-orientated future, rail announcers would be predominantly women. Their calming conciliatory voices less likely to provoke disgruntled barks from commuters pacing up and down platforms. Public-address systems were improving all the time too. One day, reports of mechanical failure or 'leaves on the line' would not be relayed by Daleks but by the clear fluty diction of voices you could fall in love with.

He probably wouldn't be back – not even to visit. Unfortunately, the feminization of public-service announcements hadn't been extended to the rolling stock. Modern trains to him were just cheap and filthy asexual steel coils. That's why, when dragging pen across paper in the office, he'd never drawn modern trains. He sketched real trains; the *Scotsman*, the *Orient Express*. Trains like the old prairie tanks with bold heraldic insignia that pumped and cut through wind and rain like men. Or trains like ladies, gliding gracefully from country village to town, wiggling around hills into view with liveries sparkling like a Hollywood starlet's grand entrance.

At home, three miles from the nearest rail line, Clive prepared to paint real trains. He took a final look into the box, knowing it would never look as pristine again. Like toothpaste, the fat tubes once squeezed and half emptied would look shabby. Moreover, the palette stained by stubborn pigments, and virgin brushes scumbled through soft paint onto hard paper, couldn't retain the enticing possibilities of that moment at the front-room table; the moment before the journey begins.

Five weeks later Clive surveyed his paintings, comparing them to the photos and reproduction oils in his *Age of Steam* book.

'The patronizing buggers.'

He thought back to his *Flying Scotsman* in New Street and the praise from the girls: 'Lovely; we ought to put it on the wall.' He thought the sketch would probably now be in the bin or, if allowed to remain in public view, be an object of derision. New staff being shown around the office would see: 'Water cooler to the right, fire exit straight ahead and, mustn't forget, Clive's picture on the wall by the window. Look at the chimney on it, and the wheels – none of them are round. If Picasso had designed trains that's what they'd have looked like! Ha!'

Clive stared at his pictures, then out of the bay window. A revelatory sadness roamed through him. He was complete rubbish at drawing and painting trains.

Having cancelled his planned trip to the Severn Valley Railway, he spent a couple of profitless days trying to re-create the homemade pies his wife used to bake. He hadn't been too bothered when his wife of forty-one years upped and went to live with her sister in Kidderminster rather than face the prospect of him after his retirement. Though she'd been gone for a couple of years now, ever since he'd reached sixty it had started: 'Well, I don't know what you'll be like when you stop going out to work. I don't want you here all day under my feet.'

He was, in truth, just as relieved he wouldn't have to spend his retirement with her. After a momentary pre-marital glow she ceased being a lady. She hadn't sparkled or glided since she'd come out of the maternity ward with their first. Though to be fair she did a damn good pie, and Clive regretted she hadn't left the recipe pinned up somewhere in the kitchen.

Attending the afternoon dance class at the local Adult Education Centre wasn't the best of ideas. Clive put on his smart suit; slate grey with the vaguest hint of a blue check in the weave. He creamed his hair; slate grey with the vaguest hint of black in the wave.

He found the right room and opened double doors into something that looked like his mother's parlour get-togethers from post-war austerity. He listened to the music, being done no favours by the tinny CD player that spat it out. A couple of men with noses raised at 45-degree angles took turns to walk – not dance – with a collection of elderly women, their cackling at the end of each dance drowning out the start of the next tune. None of the women looked under ninety and all of them looked like extras from a Hammer horror graveyard sequence.

Clive had expected the women to be ladies, like the ladies he jigged with at the Aston in his youth. Older now of course, but still slim and fresh. He'd expected a jive, not a zombie march, to the fuzzy big band stabs of budget-priced Glenn Miller. A group of crypt kickers waded towards him, one or two dangling cigarettes from colourless lips. He gulped – 'Wrong class' – and strode urgently out into the foyer, collecting a brochure as he fled.

In the front room, painting box snapped shut on the table, twisted representations of locomotives shoved out of sight in the hope that when they next saw daylight they might look like real trains, Clive flicked through the brochure.

There were hundreds of classes available all over Birmingham; in schools and colleges, community and leisure centres. The range of courses appeared infinite. You could do anything from Horse Management to Yachting. He scrutinized page after page looking for the class 'Pies like your absent wife used to bake' – without success. He noticed a couple of art classes and ringed them with a biro.

Clive enrolled and at nine-thirty on Tuesday morning found himself at a square formation of Formica-topped tables in a large airy room. Inside the square, on an isolated wooden desk, was a large vase overflowing with stalks, leaves and flowers; today's subject.

The class tutor, Jaspar, a supply teacher trying to get out of comprehensive schools and into lecturing, introduced Clive. The class consisted of eleven other people. The men: Harry, an autistic youth who produced meticulous cityscapes of the buildings outside; a fiftyish salesman who painted horses the way Clive painted trains; and another recently retired man given a watercolour kit by his daughter to have something to occupy his time and not get under his wife's feet. The women: housewives mostly called Jan, treating the class as little more than a glorified coffee and gossip morning; plus a few pensioners mostly called Ann, thankfully none resembling the ballroom dancers. Finally, directly across the desks facing him, her head partially obscured by exploding hollyhocks, Veronica.

A personable lot, they all waved and smiled, except for Veronica. She waved, smiled – and radiated.

The group had been meeting for a couple of months, though some of the pensioners had been attending various watercolour classes there for years. Jaspar noted Clive's interest and remarked that of all the subjects to attempt, trains, and particularly old steam engines, were among the most difficult to execute. However, if he'd bring in some photos they could run through it: 'We'll work on proportions. If the proportions are correct you'll find the general look will be pretty accurate.'

By the time Clive had begun streaking green, yellow and blue across his sheet of paper he had forgotten all about trains. Instead, he was thinking about that female face beyond the jut of horticulture.

He tried to store the still life in his mind, then crook a wiry neck down to the cream sheet trying to reproduce the evaporating image. In reality, though, he was peering straight through the glass vase so when his head went back to the paper he was staring into an oval face tapering at the chin. He was seeing pastel-decorated lids forming a hood over hazel eyes, a nose thin and hookish like white alabaster, cheeks delicately rouged, lips hued synthetic red. And not just any red, a wildfire of a red that reduced everything else in the room to tertiary gloom.

Chris, the salesman, offered condolences. 'Not bad for a first go. Still, we all have to start somewhere. That purpley-orange bit there looks like a pair of woman's lips. Hee! Hee! Hee!'

Clive eased his painting, already crinkling owing to the paper not being stretched properly beforehand, into his new satchel. Everyone was packing up, chattering about family or the afternoon's chores, or commenting on one another's work.

'Isn't that a beautiful colour, carmine?'

'No, permanent rose. Your petals are lovely.'

Clive watched Veronica's lips open and close as the words came out: 'Your petals are lovely' delivered with far more enthusiasm than the petals warranted. A gentle voice, though. A ladylike voice suffused with more youthful delight than many a youth could muster. He studied her as she heaped her stuff into a leather portfolio. Her hair, white and feathery like a Burmese cat's fur, crept economically around her head, short spiky strands from crown to temple, longer strands sprinkling down her neck to the collar of a fluffy dark sweater. He observed her move out of the room. She was tiny, no more than five foot tall in her wedge heels and, judging by those legs tightened by black lycra slacks, no more than a size six.

Clive freed himself from Chris, who'd been seeking a companion for the bookies, and followed Veronica up the road towards the bus stops. As they boarded there were smiles, during the journey there was conversation, and by the time she got off Veronica was Vee. A widow, sixty-four years old but with the sort of age-resistant features that made it easy to imagine how she looked at forty, thirty, even twenty – when she would have danced at places like the Aston. He got off a few stops on. It hadn't been the right bus for him and he had a mile or so to walk home, but he didn't mind. Vee was a real lady and he would muse as he walked.

Clive's first efforts at capturing Vee were equivalent to his efforts at steam engines. He wasn't deterred. He bought books on portraiture, following exercises in creating a likeness from a dissected oval. Over the weeks he gradually began to produce something that looked less like a Teletubby and more like a human being, and eventually a likeness of Vee emerged. He was pleased. He'd take it along to show her.

At the class she pored over the picture of herself while he hovered nervously, unsure how she'd react.

'My God! How can you just do that, without me even being there?'

He thought it best not to mention the finished picture, pencil with a faint wash, was attempt number twenty-seven.

Jaspar noted the construction that underpinned the port-rait. 'You can apply that principle to trains too.'

'Trains? Hmm, I think I may stick to people in future.'

Vee invited Clive round to her maisonette afterwards. She wanted him to show her how to get a likeness from a dissected oval. He followed her up the front garden path watching her Lilliputian bottom and legs gliding, wiggling. A ferocity of thought rushed through his mind. His arms around her nymph waist, his mouth glued to her lipstick pout, naked bodies creased and scarified by longevity pushing and pulling inside one another. But it was just a thought.

Vee went into the kitchen, leaving him perched on her sofa, barely an inch of him touching upholstery in that awkward posture new visitors adopt when told to make themselves at home in unfamiliar rooms. The lounge was as its owner, small and tidy. She called him for tea and grilled chicken with vegetables. They ate and talked until Vee asked for the drawing lesson. He took out his A4 sketch-book and tugged the last sheet from its spiral-bound cover.

'You've run out of paper, Clive. Are these any good?'

She opened the shelving unit above the washing machine and took out an expensive-looking vinyl-covered sketch-book. He saw the entire unit was crammed with art materials. There was tube upon tube of paint, big 225ml tubes of oil right down to 8ml tubes of watercolour. Stacked next to them were pans and half-pans of solid cake paint. Brushes; she had skinny riggers and fat filberts with gold stamped lettering along the handles. In a corner were paper blocks and canvas boards. Poking out here and there was other stuff; bottles and things sealed in plastic. Scarcely any of it seemed to have been used.

'You could open your own art shop with that lot. Where do you keep the four-foot by two-foot gilt frames then?'

Clive half expected her to explain the equipment belonged to a family member. They were possibly an artistic lot, but there were clearly no other residents in the maisonette.

'I really should stop getting this stuff. I hardly use any of it, but I can't resist a bargain.'

He picked up a couple of tubes. 'I've read about this acrylic paint.'

'Take them; I don't like them. They dry out before you can put a stroke onto paper.'

He offered to pay.

She smiled at the smattering of coins he tried to pass her. 'That's far too much. Now how about that lesson?'

Clive drew an oval, dissecting it vertically and horizontally through the middle. He sketched circles for eyes through the horizontal line, then parallels on which the facial features could rest vertically. It looked like a Teletubby until he placed eyebrows and, below, heavy eyelids, sockets and pupils. He drew a hookish nose and buried the exposed cranium with light feathery pencil lines. And there she was: Vee.

'Wow! It looks so simple.'

She told him to hang on while she dashed into the lounge to fetch a photo from the mantelpiece. She stood it on the table. 'Can you do one of Callum?'

He tried. The hair looked okay but the face was still Vee. Another sheet of paper and Clive scratched and flicked his 2B lead. He grimaced. Vee's grandson looked like a gargoyle with a boyband haircut. It hadn't occurred to him before, but it had taken dozens of efforts to catch a likeness of Vee and once he had it he didn't want to let it go. She was the only thing he wanted to draw.

'I'd better not let him see that, not if I want him to do the decorating again.' She laughed.

He felt foolish but cheered up when Vee asked if they

could go somewhere the following day. She suggested Walsall Art Gallery. Some of the pictures were a bit strange but she promised to take him to the shop where she got bargain art materials.

Clive extracted every last protruding hair from his nostrils and ears, ironed his most youthful shirt and brushed his suit. It was a date after all. What would Vee be wearing? A designer lilac trouser suit with big lapels and flowing flares to accentuate her glide, or a stretchy black pencil skirt with camel blazer?

What Vee was wearing when she answered the door was a big floppy brown felt hat and an ankle-length Afghan coat, each shoulder criss-crossed by an enormous canvas bag. 'You look smart,' she smirked. Vee looked good too, albeit in a different way. The coat was tight and dug into her in an almost sculptural fashion.

They bussed it into Walsall and she locked her arm into his as they moved along the high street. Lads of all ages glanced, unsure if what was under the floppy hat was sixteen or sixty-four. As for Clive, he had his 'first date' face on. The one you see people wearing when everything is still a jumble of feverish imaginings.

Both agreed the coffee in the café was the best thing about the art gallery, though some of the Garman Ryan collection was nice. As for the modern stuff upstairs, well, it was just like trains. The brutes had taken over with their pursuit of the new and urban at the expense of the old and Arcadian.

Back in the town centre Vee led Clive into an art shop. He drifted around examining things. Then he saw the prices and quickly put them down again. 'Did you get your materials during a sale, Vee? These don't seem very cheap at all.'

She tilted the brim of her hat, checked the female assistant on the phone at the far counter wasn't watching, and scooped a number of items off a lower shelf into one of her bags. Clive's face contorted into a prizeworthy gurn and a jolt propelled him one step sideways. He stood transfixed, flushing, then moved towards the door, stopping only to beam at the unsuspecting assistant, who politely upturned her mouth in return.

Outside in cooler air, he felt cold beads of sweat under his arms as Vee, giggling, marched him off to the bus station. He didn't speak on the way home, afraid to utter a word in case other passengers overheard. They got off at Vee's stop.

In her kitchen, Vee's giggle grew louder and louder until it became an uncontrolled howl while he stood there quivering.

'Clive, stop looking at me like that!'

She handed over the ill-gotten gains: a selection of tube paints. The colours were new to him; alizarin crimson, raw sienna and a green he couldn't pronounce.

'I can't accept these. Veronica, do you think you might have a problem? You can't just . . .'

'Kleptomania. No, I don't have a problem. But isn't it wicked, deliciously so.'

She hung her big floppy hat on the kitchen-door hook. 'Hang on, I'll be back in a tick.'

He guiltily held the paints while glancing into the lounge through a crack in the door. The Afghan coat was flung across an armchair and Vee vanished into her bedroom in her cork mules – just her cork mules. She hadn't been wearing anything else.

Clive coughed and hurled himself out of the maisonette. He galloped home, only realizing when he was safely in his hallway that he had stolen property in his pockets.

*

It was deliciously wicked. Clive: Maoist cap flattening his quiff, the inaugural bristles of a goatee poking through his chin, huge serge greatcoat; and Vee in her hat and coat clinging to him. The pair looked like Stop the War marchers – from the Vietnam war, that is.

They went to Coventry by train, visiting the Herbert Gallery to buy coffee and nick books. They went to Stratford, eating cakes at Anne Hathaway's cottage and smuggling calligraphy sets out of WH Smiths. Birmingham, Wolverhampton, Bilston, they did them all, those two light-fingered bohemians. And her with nothing on under her coat.

New Clive still painted portraits of Vee. He cleared his bookshelf of train, aviation and old speedway books to accommodate the painting materials he'd been pinching over the last few months. His abilities with watercolour improved. The new sable brushes coated in quality pigment just flowed across luxurious Bockingford paper. He learned how to add cool and warm shadows. The pictures were good. They physically looked like her.

But they were the Vee he had first encountered at the art class; the lady, not the elemental force. These portraits, built in stages from pencil through to finishing gouache highlights, simply weren't the real Vee: the Vee of mischief.

To make more space he opened the drawer his old pictures were stored in with the intention of throwing out the unkeepable. Virtually everything in there was Vee in some form. Vee with eyes too big, Vee with a nose like a triangle, Vee looking like an older Ulrika Jonsson; that one made him wonder.

Curled up in embarrassment at the bottom of the drawer was his first picture from the art class with its clumsy puddles and blooms of paint spread into each other. However, Clive could see within the hotchpotch a pair of purpley-orange lips, swirls forming a hookish nose, and two watery brown buds floating in petals. Unmistakably those eyes, those shoplifting eyes, elusive normally but captured perfectly here. He stared at it until the room began to darken, realizing he'd had her essence in that drawer all along.

The class still met on Tuesday mornings, apart from Chris who had left to join Monday evening's digital photography. They still painted still lifes, flowers or fruit, sometimes wine and cognac bottles. Once every few weeks, much to the delight of the Jans and Anns, one of Jaspar's broke student mates would come in to model. Clive always produced something that looked like a gargoyle: he'd have been a sensation in the Gothic period. Vee was the only reason he kept attending. His interest in drawing and painting had long ceased to include representational watercolours. At home he squirted spectral twirls and gouged and scraped, spread with palette knife and fingers. He placed iridescent white to make irises and lips glisten, and when exhaustion ended the session, she was looking back up at him.

He hadn't shown Vee any of these pictures. Would she be able to see herself in the firmament? He needed to find out so he decided he would show her after their next shoplifting expedition, or he would have done had they not been caught.

The out-of-town family-run shop specialized in framing, had a printing facility and a small retail unit with a maze of aisles that stocked art and craft materials. A range far more extensive than the shop's small size suggested. The shelves were about six foot high, perfect for Clive to stand on tiptoes and peer over like a watchful meerkat while the little minx whisked the contents of a lower shelf into her canvas bags.

Though he could keep surveillance on one daughter at the till, he didn't spot a second strolling up the carpet-floored aisle to refill the technical pens section. She'd been sternly observing them. He stepped down off his haunches and turned straight into her glare. He experienced the same shame as all that time ago in Walsall. Sweat forming in droplets under his cap, his face feeling like it was turning the colour of a postbox. Vee poked up the brim of her hat.

'Oh no! It's not her fault,' she yelped. 'We're not supposed to be out without supervision. She won't get into trouble, will she?'

Clive stared at Vee. She was starting to cry. The daughter, severity melting into uneasy bemusement, muttered, 'Who won't get into trouble?'

'The nurse, at the home. She'll get the blame – not us. And she's got a young family. It's terrible.'

By now the scene had been swelled by the daughter from the till, a son emerging from the framing room, and the mother who owned the shop. The family looked at the quaking Clive and the blubbering Vee.

'You should lock us up. Don't take it out on her. She doesn't know we're here. We should be back there playing cards, watching *Countdown*.'

Dumbfounded, the family looked at one another. Vee tipped up the canvas bag so its contents dropped onto the carpet. There were erasers, stencils, plastic geometry instruments and a dozen or so tubes of fabric paint – all lemon yellow.

'Take it all back. I don't want any of it. It's the tablets. It isn't me.'

The family looked at the booty, then looked at one anther again, then looked at Clive and Vee.

The bus trip home, like their first time, was made in silence. Clive put the kettle on and arched his neck to see her coat being slung onto the lounge chair and her naked body slink into the bedroom. She returned, clothed, moments later to be handed a cup of extra strong tea.

Clive shook his head, expelling every bit of air he could locate. 'That . . . that was some performance, Vee. So . . . spontaneous.'

'Mmm, it was rather good, even if I say so myself. Much better than the last time.'

'What?'

'I got my words all mixed up. Nerves. I thought they were going to take my details. Course that was before I met you.'

'Vee, how many times have you been caught?'

'That was the fourth. The second time they made me pay for the stuff. The sauce of them. And it was all rubbish.'

Vee went to the hob to stir-fry. Clive looked into his satchel. He might as well show her the picture.

'It's not supposed to be an exact likeness, more of a . . . response.'

She held the board up to the light, then placed it on the table, squinting at the acrylic dollops and streaks. 'It's like pictures I've seen in books and galleries. I don't know how you can look at me and see all those colours. I love it. Can I keep it?'

She leaned over and kissed his cheek; for the first time her wildfire-red lips had touched him. There was a look. But it was just a look.

Clive had taken her face as far as he could without leaving human features behind altogether. Now he wanted to capture what he had glimpsed through the crack in the door. Covering his front-room floor with sheets of news-papers he laid out a series of fourteen-by-ten-inch white canvas boards in a perpendicular row fastened together with strips of masking tape. He squirted entire tubes of paint and scattered glasses of water onto the surfaces and modelled shapes and textures and features. He put paint on, scraped it off. He rubbed off calm tones to sling down untamed ones. He worked for days, missing the class.

Vee phoned. She'd decided to stop shoplifting, reckoning you could only get caught so often before magistrates became involved. That could mean her daughters fussing, moralizing, trying to make her act her age. She didn't want to be warden-controlled by her own kids, not yet anyway. Clive arranged a meeting for Monday morning. He had a new picture to show her.

Vee watched him tip out his bag. He took her hat off the door, scattered the boards on the table, reaching for the one with hooks and wire first. He put that up, then attached a second with tape. More followed until a life-size nude hung down. Vee saw her face in the top panel, her twisting back and an angular arm in the second, light-bulb buttocks in the next, swirling knees and legs in another. She moved closer to the door.

'God!'

'Just God?' asked Clive.

'I'd love to feel like that,' she said, running fingertips over the impudent storm of paint.

So, just before the evening's classes were about to finish, Clive and Vee walked through the gates of the Adult Education Centre. He needed both hands to carry his packed satchel as they roamed corridors looking for rooms unlocked, unlit. They found one and crouched in a recess to wait. At ten past nine the room was illuminated briefly by a slice of light from the corridor. The door closed; just closed. Good, he wouldn't have to break the lock with the screwdriver he'd brought along. They stood at the windows to watch cars moving away; the gridlock of students followed by a trickle of tutors, then finally the caretaker's van stopping to padlock the gates. When he'd gone they knew they were alone.

They found the art room and switched on the lights. Clive heaved the contents of his satchel onto his usual table. The room was still arranged in a square with the desk in the centre. That was moved and a big single-masted easel pushed into its place. Vee looked up.

'Now?'

'Yes, Vee.'

Vee took off her floppy hat and her coat. She leaned against the easel to inch off her shoes. Clive gulped so hard he could almost feel his Adam's apple in the roof of his mouth as she stood there naked, radiant.

'Clive?'

He had to put away the wave of thoughts rushing through his mind. He lifted her up, his perspiring palms slipping and losing grip of her malleable body. He felt like an angler trying hard to land the big fish or, more appropriately, the tiny mermaid. He hoisted her up onto the easel, tied her ankles with cord and secured both arms behind her head on the mast. She was ready; a primed canvas.

He tried to walk casually to the aluminium sink, but lolloped like an over-excited teen. He filled bowls with water and turpentine and scattered paint of every description across the table. There were full tubes of oil and gouache, pans of watercolour and, of course, the half-used acrylics that had created Vee on his front-room floor.

He was tentative at first. A body colour of diluted raw sienna dabbed on with a mop brush with a thicker mix of cadmium red added to catch warm shadows. He looked for cooler tones; cobalt blue patted with a sponge and phthalo green smeared on with a rag.

Gaining confidence, he picked up tubes of alizarin crimson

and ultramarine, squirting them gesturally onto her skin, until there was no skin, just paint.

Her eyes glazed over. She nodded, white upper teeth clamped tightly around her bottom lip as he began to model her face with his fingers, defining planes with smooth streaks. He dashed to and from the table grabbing colours.

He moved paint around her contours and crevices *alla prima*, reds into yellows into greens into blues. Thinner mixes finding their own routes over heavy impasto layers.

Vee blinked wildly, breathed quickly. Her eyes and mouth were the only parts of her not entombed in pigment.

'God! This is so . . .' she said.

A voice so comfortable that Clive thought for a second: It can't be like the shoplifting, can it? Surely she hasn't done this before?

The torrent of paint continued. Wrong colours were wiped and replaced with the right ones; Vee's colours. Eventually the sweat-drenched Clive was finished, and Vee was finished. Her face, her breasts, her stomach, her thighs, her calves all moulded into a Fauvist rage.

She laughed mischievously. He stepped back, feeling a spasm and a warm white lava from his limp tingling penis fill his underwear and soak the front of his trousers. 'Oh no!' he groaned. Turning to conceal the mishap from Vee, he trod in a pool of spilt turpentine which in his present unbalanced state sent him sliding across the room. His legs stopped when he came to the sink but his upper body carried on and his head carried on even further, right into the taps. He dropped to the floor, all crumpled up and moaning.

And then he stopped moaning and was just all crumpled up.

Vee called, 'Clive?' Then, 'Clive!' Then, 'CLIVE!!!'

*

'Clive? Clive! CLIVE!!!'

He started to regain consciousness, rubbing his throbbing forehead and focusing slowly on spears of sunlight coming through the blinds. Vee was still on the easel, unable to move but mumbling about what her daughters would make of all this. He heard other voices calling out his name. Thankfully not angels at the gates of heaven, but who then?

Looking at the doorway he saw them all: Harry, the Jans and Anns, and Jaspar who had just opened up for Tuesday morning art class.

Joe Stalin's Ape

John Mulcreevy

Screaming police vehicles jerked into the mouth of the underpass. Some had red and yellow markings, some blue and lime. No two seemed to have the same pattern so, littered at random, they blended to give the appearance of an enormous Peruvian blanket. If you didn't know they were attending a road accident, you'd have thought they'd caused it.

A middle-aged sergeant with that affected swagger that brings to mind John Wayne – or haemorrhoids – went swaggering over to the squashed car. 'No casualties,' he roared into his walkie-talkie, describing a white Audi against the tunnel wall, and a few yards behind a minivan with a silver Hyundai rammed into the back of it. He opened his notebook and licked his pencil.

The Audi had been forced to swerve into the wall. The minivan behind slammed on the brakes to avoid her, but the Hyundai hadn't been so alert. Nice and straightforward, so he thought, until he asked what had caused her to swerve.

'Well, I could see this thing rattling on top of the vehicle in front, Constable,' said the Audi driver.

'Sergeant, actually.'

'Yes, sorry. Humongous thing it was.'

'Humongous,' he wrote.

'Then all of a sudden it sprang to life as it went into the tunnel and its arm seemed to break off against the wall and came flying towards me, hit my bonnet and . . .' She paused for breath and pointed at her car. 'Well . . .'

Had it been Saturday night he'd have been gesturing for the breathalyser, but it was still early afternoon.

'And what exactly was it that sprang to life?'

She prodded her glasses against the bridge of her nose. 'It looked like a gorilla.'

He quoted from his notes into his radio: 'It appears there was something that looked like a gorilla in a . . . yeah, Gor-rill-la. Eh? Well, I don't know if it was driving or not.'

The minivan driver came over. 'Don Lucas, Harvey's Pressings. It was certainly a giant gorilla. And it had something coming out of its ars – bottom.'

The copper's pencil snapped in two. 'Shit!'

'No, it was more like music.'

'Y'know. I think it was them Sugababes,' added his mate.

He snuggled back into his walkie-talkie. 'It appears this, er, gorilla was emitting pop music from its backside. What? Are you extracting the . . . all right then, we think it was the Sugababes.'

The Hyundai driver tapped him on the shoulder. 'You've got that all wrong.'

There might be a bit of common sense from this one, the sergeant thought.

'It was definitely Girls Aloud. The new single – my missus has it on all the time.'

Everyone in the cul-de-sac got on all right with each other. Joe Stalin often sat on the garden wall of the empty house on the corner nodding benignly at women and kids as they came and went. The men of the cul-de-sac he'd beckon over to share home-brew and jam tarts. Dale didn't touch booze but had a sweet tooth and they were decent enough tarts. His mate Kelly reckoned the tarts were a bit off, but he liked the free ale served up in cracked white TUC mugs from a plastic industrial disinfectant container. It had a nozzle that could pour or spray: spraying being better for a good frothy head. He'd quickly guzzle the brew, then smack his lips and blurt out, 'Ahh, a heady elixir. Get Mrs Stal – um, your good lady wife to bring us more.'

Sometimes, when visiting their aunt at number 8, the Younghusband twins would join them, both sitting on the wall with one leg outstretched, the other tucked in. Danny would take a mug but Mick wouldn't. 'Dunno about that, mate. Smells like the stuff they use to strip paint with.'

That would, no doubt, be down to the secret ingredient Joe would never discuss.

The provision of food and drink was hardly done for altruistic reasons. Once an audience was present, Joe Stalin would go on and on.

'I was down the dole and there were these two bright sparks, baseball hats, speaking in slow motion. You've seen 'em around. Moaning about this African who was taking ages to do his forms they were. Bloody great, I thought. If you don't like 'em over here then vote in a bloody government that'll sell their country tractors instead of fighter planes.'

Mick looked at his watch; he'd have to go, he worked nights. Dale left with him; he wanted a word about a new cooker. Joe didn't mind; Kelly and Danny were still there.

'The way to stop them exporting all our jobs is to export the gaffers instead. Competitive global market. Cobblers! See how they fancy living ten to a room on a bowl of rice.'

Kelly swilled the bottom of his mug. 'I was thinking. Could you get us a couple of gallons of this?'

'That good, eh,' smirked Joe.

Kelly knew a decorator who'd like to try it.

Joe's wife opened the cupboard under the kitchen sink and pulled out a full container of the home-brew for him.

'Thanks, Mrs Pooley.'

From the window Kelly looked out over the back garden. 'Joe, what's that on the lawn?'

'Come on, I'll show you.'

They stood at a large frame made from twisted wire coat-hangers lying flat on the grass.

'You know what it is, don't you?'

Kelly rubbed his chin. 'Something to get rid of crows?'

'Piss orf! It's . . .'

Dale put the tray of drinks down on the table in the Legion. Kelly flicked up beermats, catching them in one hand.

'Cheers, Dale mate. So he told me what it was and, well, I remember it from yonks ago. Looked nothing like it, but I didn't want to say anything. I flogged his home-brew, y'know.'

Dale drank his orange juice. 'He said he's going to cover it and paint it.'

'What for?'

'Reckons he's going to take it home. You getting a last round in?'

Fishing a grubby handkerchief and a few coins from his pocket – not enough for a round – Kelly enquired, 'Home where?'

'I'll tell you another time. Want some chips? That cooker Mick's got me does a bangin' chip.'

On the way home they spotted Joe carrying bulging black bin bags into his house.

'Oi! You doing that the right way round? Most people put their bags out,' snorted Dale.

'I'm going through them for the paper,' Joe replied, hunching up furtively.

'Come and have some chips.'

They were good chips. Dale's old cooker had a dodgy ignition and just the one setting which resulted in chips being hot as the Sahara on the outside and cold as the Arctic in the middle. These, though, were great. Joe had fetched over another of his containers. Dale wanted to know when the frame was going to be covered and painted. Joe said he was planning to start when he'd got hold of some paste. Dale grinned impishly. 'Kelly's decorator mate will sort you out with some; probably do a deal in exchange for more of that home-brew.'

Kelly uttered 'Uh!' and gave one of those looks that says, I've just been shafted here.

So, they began dunking old newspapers and cardboard into buckets of paste to slap onto the wire frame. Within a couple of hours they'd used up all the paper Joe had taken from his neighbours' bags. The frame had three fingers finished.

'It'll take for ever to cover a thing this size with paper,' moaned Kelly, wiping his sticky hands on the grass.

Later, in the kitchen, Dale ate a couple of tarts. Kelly didn't want any of the previously irresistible home-brew so Joe sprayed just the one mugful for himself. It was agreed they needed a good constant supply of wastepaper. Joe's weekly consumption consisted of one freesheet, Friday's *Morning Star* and a couple of lasagne boxes. Combined with what he found elsewhere in the cul-de-sac, his creation would be fleshed out a rate of about five inches a week – and there were an awful lot of inches to be covered. The wire frame was ten foot long and its arm span almost the same.

'Leave it with us,' said Dale.

*

Kelly's rusty old Astra chugged up to Joe's gate, crammed full of papers, magazines, catalogues and directories; string held the boot down, though several sheets still fluttered out and off down the road. In the front, Dale's hairline was the only part of him visible behind the wodge balanced on his lap.

'You've got about a leg's worth there,' he stated proudly as he pushed the door open and dumped the wodge on the pavement. Kelly got out and they began taking armfuls into the back garden.

'Where'd you get all that lot from?' gasped Joe in disbelief.

'The recycling tank by the school. We sifted out the cans and half-eaten sausage rolls before we loaded up.'

Joe patted them both on the shoulders as they unloaded. They had the materials. Now they needed a workforce.

Mick Younghusband loaned out his two kids, who brought their friends, and by the weekend the garden teemed with constructional activity. A couple of kids stirred paste in a concrete mixer Kelly had scrounged off a builder mate. They stirred with a plastic fan rake, picking out solidifying lumps to throw at the ones dipping paper into paste buckets.

Other youngsters, under Joe's strict guidance, moulded the soggy stuff onto the horizontal frame; beginning with the feet, moving up towards bent knees.

'Blimey! You've used most of that paper up already,' said Kelly later in the evening.

Joe wanted to know if they could get him some more.

The next two raids on the green metal tank were carried out successfully, but on the third they spotted the unmistakable, unmissable bright yellow jackets of police community support officers.

'Oh brilliant! Banana peelers.'

Given time to think, they could probably have bluffed their way out of what was hardly a heinous offence. They could claim to be searching for a lost lottery ticket or collecting coupons for a commemorative plate. Instead, Kelly suggested they hide inside the tank. He managed, with a push from Dale, to get both legs in, but the gap was far too small for a grown man. Fortunately, the support officers carried on patrolling the opposite side of the road. If they'd crossed over they would have noticed one bloke seemingly trying to recycle another.

Joe hooted when he heard Kelly's explanation for the hobbling. There were even more kids in the garden now. A few teenagers, attracted by the home-brew's reputation, had taken to coming along, not that they did much work. The girls wouldn't touch anything covered in paste and the lads, two skateboarders, built a ramp on the rockery where they practised switch flip tricks between shots of brew.

'It's like double snakebite with a gobful of chillis,' enthused the one in the tight beanie and baggy everything else.

'Who are they?' grunted Joe.

'That one, he's Ixy. That's short for Icarus: King of Flight.'

'I'll give him flight if he don't get off my rockery.'

Those two might come in useful, thought Kelly. 'I ain't going near that tank again. Nearly amputated me walking gear it did.'

The ringing came after midnight. Joe blearily staggered down the stairs as his doorbell was repeatedly pressed. He unbolted, unchained and unlocked.

'What the f –'

'Nice pyjamas, Mr Stalin. Hurr! Hurr!' Ixy and his mate, Nosegrinder, were trying to avoid sniggering too much at Joe's pink pyjamas.

'What do you two want?'

'We've got your paper. That Jerome Kelly geezer said you wanted it round here, but we can't get it in.'

Joe peered around the corner of his gable to see the recycling tank balanced on a skateboard partway through his garden gate.

'Jesus wept! Not the whole flamin' thing – just the paper. I only wanted just the paper.'

Ixy shrugged his shoulders, telling Joe it was quicker to bring the whole tank than make loads of trips with bundles of wastepaper under their arms. Joe told them to get the paper out and then take the tank back.

'That Kelly geezer said there'd be a tenner in it for us.'

Joe responded with a glare, a very icy glare.

'A fiver each then?' tried Nosegrinder.

Slam!

The kids rapidly emptied out the paper and pushed the tank back up the path.

'It's a lot lighter now, innit.'

'Yeah. When we get on the main road we'll give it a good shove, Ixy.'

They awkwardly manoeuvred out of the cul-de-sac. Each time a wheel hit an uneven paving slab the tank would either rock noisily or scrape against the ground. On the main road Ixy took imaginary measurements.

'It's a good slope so if we let it roll we should be able to get it back outside the school, no probs.'

They positioned themselves, backs against the tank, aiming to control the descent with their feet. And it worked – for a few yards. Then they just couldn't stop the momentum and were forced to jump out of the way to allow the tank to find its own trajectory. It rumbled and clattered down the road, glancing against a tree, which upset the balance, causing the board to weave erratically rather than roll smoothly. It must have just missed a foraging cat, for there was a godforsaken shriek, and then tank hit kerb. The skateboard flew up and the tank overturned with a deafening clang in the middle of a zebra crossing. Ixy snatched his board and they scarpered down a side road before the locals began pouring out of their houses to see where the earthquake was.

On the rockery, Joe repeatedly jabbed a finger at the free-sheet article about vandals blocking a main road with a re-cycling tank. He was particularly angry about the quotes.

'Listen to this. "Mindless vandals . . . at a time when the community is showing enormous interest in recycling . . ." Load of cobblers!'

Joe pointed out he was doing more than anyone to get rid of unwanted paper in a productive way. 'Besides, what do the Environmental do with it? Pulp it and turn it into leaflets telling people to recycle!'

He scrunched up the freesheet and marched over to the paste bucket, dunked it vigorously, then spread it onto the buttocks of the frame. Ixy pulled a glum face. He'd wanted to keep that article for his bedroom wall.

The Younghusband children and their friends became ridiculously fervent about the project. They asked neighbours to donate scrap paper and cardboard; even the school had a special collection. Mini paper Everests sprang up all over the garden. Mrs Pooley couldn't get her washing out, but she put up with it. At least he had a hobby. Though, more than once she was heard complaining about what he got up to in the spare bedroom.

It wasn't just old paper that found its way into the garden. The woman delivering freesheets came away from one house to find her trolley emptied and a couple of skateboarders whizzing off, bundles under each arm. Danny,

never the most mature of the twins, produced a wheel-
barrow full of books, singing, 'Libraries gave us papier
mâché,' to the tune of that Manic Street Preachers song.

The frame was becoming recognizable as some sort of
monster. Layer after layer of covering gave it the appearance of an anatomically bizarre Egyptian mummy. The
head hadn't been done yet. Joe was supposed to be doing
that himself; instead he sat idling on the rockery.

'The dole sent me round to this place. Bloody great, the
gaffer wasn't much older than those kids.'

'Reckon you'll ever work again?' asked Dale.

Joe shook his head. 'There's no proper jobs for us any
more. Not since they smashed the unions. No one to stick
up for us and we don't stick up for ourselves.'

Dale edged away while Joe just carried on, his booming
polemic drifting over the kids' heads. 'They put us all on
the dole cos there's no unions for claimants. That's why
they got rid of the jobs: to get rid of the unions.'

Ixy tried a switch flip on his board. Joe bellowed, 'Oi,
Dale! Come and tell this young 'un how it used to be when
we had Robbo and Arthur sticking up for us.'

Dale humoured him. 'We could do with a revolution,
couldn't we, Joe?'

'Flamin' right we could. I'll tell you something. If they'd
tried flogging off Rover in them days we'd have brought
the bloody government down.'

'What did you do then when you had a job?' enquired
Ixy.

Joe puffed out his chest. 'I was a pipe fitter, me.'

'Sounds boring, that. I'd rather be on the dole like you
now, building monsters and drinking that mad shit. Awesome!'

Eventually they finished the papier-mâché gorilla and
painted black emulsion over the front of the rough paper

flesh. Joe himself placed two ping-pong balls for the eyes and painted a row of bright white teeth. They left it to dry for a couple of hours, then Ixy and Nosegrinder turned it over to do the back.

Joe and Dale began tidying up. The lawn was wrecked and there were shreds of chewed paper everywhere; stuck to plants like origami blossoms, hanging from branches like artificial leaves and smeared over the path like chalkstone inserts. Kelly put the mixer and some buckets by the gate. The only thing missing was Joe's old radio, left out for the youngsters to listen to. Dale noticed the kids spending a lot of time gathered around the gorilla's bottom. He wandered over for a look.

'Classic, or what?' guffawed Ixy.

'You should turn that back over. You don't want Joe Stalin to see what you've done to his ape.'

Kelly arranged to borrow a flatbed truck from a plumber mate, having agreed a fee of two gallons of drain un-blocker. It was all set for Saturday. They would transport the gorilla to Birmingham city centre, just like in the early 1970s when a tobacco company had commissioned a fibreglass King Kong for the city. It had become a bit of a landmark back then. Little kids would scratch their names on its thick legs; bigger ones would climb up and swing from its massive outstretched arms. It moved around the city for a while, then was sold off to a market in Scotland or Timbuktu or somewhere. Naturally, once it had gone it entered the local psyche through regular appearances in newspaper 'Whatever happened to?' columns, alongside the stolen FA Cup from 1895 and the current whereabouts of Benny from *Crossroads*.

'What the bloody hell is that!' Joe bellowed.

'My mate got taken ill. I couldn't get the keys for his

truck,' explained Kelly sheepishly, winding down his Astra window.

'Ill?'

'Yeah,' mumbled Kelly, 'he drank some drain unblocker.'

'What did he do that for? I let you have two gallons of home-brew for him.'

Joe stormed off to supervise the moving of the gorilla from garden to transport, or as he put it, 'That flamin' Dinky car.'

Dale looked at the front of the car and noticed the fake number plates.

'I got vibes about this,' frowned Kelly. 'I always put them on when I get vibes.'

They watched Joe, the twins and the skateboarders dragging King Kong through the garden gate. One arm dragged against the side of the house, leaving a long black smear on the rendering.

Kelly confided to Dale: 'Y'know my mate, Eddie the plumber. He says it's the best unblocker he's ever tried. I told him to only use it on drains. They rushed him to hospital last night.'

They wondered what Joe Stalin's guts must be like. They were probably rotting from the inside out. Give it a year or two and they'd be preserving him in papier mâché.

They hoisted the ape up and settled him face-down on the car roof. Ixy and Nosegrinder coerced Joe into the front passenger seat while they roped it down. Dale and Danny got in the back and the kids, sniggering guiltily, clambered in after them. There was a huge roar from the throng of gathered youngsters as Kelly twisted the key and pressed the pedal down. The car spluttered.

'Too much weight. A couple of you will have to get out.'

Joe, seething at the ignominious transport his masterpiece would be travelling on, grunted, 'Cobblers!' and stamped violently on the pedal. The clutch jerked and they chugged off.

Windows down, the kids pulled rope ends taut, Ixy tying his around his waist. Kong bumped noisily against the roof only stopping when they slowed for a red light. Joe, looking at the dashboard, asked if the radio was on. 'No,' said Kelly.

'I can hear music coming from somewhere,' said Joe, his eyes flitting from dash to visors to floor. Kelly looked in his rearview mirror to see his four passengers in various states of thinly suppressed hysteria.

The journey wasn't too hazardous provided they kept away from the kerb and veered around buses. The overhanging anthropoid arms only scraped two number 51s and a 107.

'So where exactly are we taking the chimp?' asked Kelly.

'To put it where the old King Kong was. I don't like the new Brum much,' answered Joe.

'It used to be by the old Bull Ring,' Dale said.

'That's right. That's where we're going to put it.'

Dale laughed. 'You'll be lucky. It's either a slip road or a rack of miniskirts now.'

They took the A38 round by the university. Joe shuffled uneasily. 'There's definitely music coming from somewhere.'

Danny said they ought to look out for the poster as they went through the underpass. The four in the back leaned over to see the advert with the fifteen-foot brunette and her boa constrictor. The car shuddered; Joe tried to steady himself by grabbing Kelly's knee which caused him to let go of the steering wheel, resulting in Nosegrinder losing hold of the rope as they entered the underpass. There was a crack above them and seconds later a crash behind them.

Dale peered out of the back to see a pile-up and a papier-mâché arm in the road. Kelly regained control, skidding to a halt in the dark underpass. Kong smashed down on the roof, sliding forward so he was looking straight through the windscreen at them.

Nosegrinder had been dragged halfway out of the window; only Danny's quick intervention in grabbing his waist prevented him being carried off by the G-force.

Joe got out and climbed up onto the bonnet. 'We'll have to tie it back. What the –'

'He's found it then,' announced Dale.

Joe stared at the ape's backside and heard loud pop music. He heaved himself up onto the roof and looked. A square had been cut out to make a panel and duck-taped down again. Two holes revealed grilles. He pulled off the tape and lifted the panel to see his radio wedged inside; the grilles were speakers.

'Girls Aloud there. Will they still be holding the number one spot tomorrow?'

Nosegrinder, wedged in the window, called, 'Mr Stalin, get in quick – it's the fuzz!'

A white foam of police vehicles bubbled into the underpass. There was no time to tie Kong down. Joe scrambled off the roof, tumbled down the bonnet and staggered back into his seat. Dale and Danny assisted Ixy and Nosegrinder in tugging the ropes taut again.

'I had vibes,' sighed Kelly.

The car lurched forward. There was no immediate pursuit – the underpass must be blocked.

'What are we gonna do with it now?'

'Dunno.'

'You can never find an Empire State Building when you need one,' contributed Dale.

It could have been a scene from a wildlife park: a car going along with a playful monkey on top slapping the roof. They made it to the end of the tunnel before Kelly spotted the flashing blue light.

'He'll be with us in a minute. I can't get out of second gear with that thing rattling about up there.'

There was only one thing for it. Ixy and Nosegrinder would have to climb up and steady Kong. Dale and Danny would hold them. The skateboarders needed little persuasion to get out and brave the slipstream.

'This is awesome! Better than *Grand Theft Auto*!'

The kids restrained the ape as best they could. Kelly urged his exhausted motor into third, then fourth. The kids slid their hands about, scrambling for something to grab hold of. Ixy, finding the hole left by the removed panel, stuck his hands into the gorilla's arse, inadvertently tuning into another station's cricket commentary.

The police sergeant shouted into his walkie-talkie, shouted at his driver, shouted at other motorists, and shouted above the wailing siren on top of the patrol car.

'Any cars in the vicinity of . . . hang on. Marcus! Put your foot down . . . where's that transit going . . . pull over, you stupid . . .'

Kelly, picking up speed, saw traffic in front of him pull over to allow the chase. The sergeant could see the giant gorilla on the roof and the two kids hanging from the windows. He ordered Marcus to head them off.

Dale watched through the rear windscreen. 'He's getting a bit close.'

Kelly glanced at his speedometer. He could get another ten m.p.h. out of this baby, and he went for it. But the sudden thrust was a thrust too much for Ixy. He lost hold, slithering back into the car, his foot landing in Danny's groin. Kong rocked and Nosegrinder was sucked back into the car.

The sergeant and his driver watched the ape, free of ropes and restraint, blow upright and topple over like a gymnast performing a backwards somersault. It didn't land on its feet to a rising crescendo of applause, though. It hit the road headfirst; eyes bouncing off, decapitated skull pogoing to rest in a drain. The remaining arm came off too, and the big black torso rolled to just in front of the braking police car. The coppers got out in time to hear the death throes of the mighty creature: 'Hampshire have just lost another wicket.'

Their quarry had screamed away into a maze of old industrial side roads. They had the registration number; they'd arrest him later. The sergeant turned to Marcus. 'Fancy spinning a coin for who gives evidence when this gets to court? I really don't fancy taking this one before the beak.'

The Astra plunged through bumpy roads flanked by tall deserted factories. Ixy, one part nerves, one part hyper-activity, nodded and drummed on the back seat. 'This is sick, man!'

Kelly checked the mirror. 'You ain't gonna puke in here!'

'Nah, I mean sick as in awesome. We gonna do it again?'

Kelly, Dale and Danny retorted in unison 'Are we f –'

Joe appeared pensive. 'Don't be like that. Actually . . .'

The following Saturday, much to his wife's relief, Joe brought it down from the spare bedroom and the two skater boys helped him take the life-size papier-mâché model of militant 1970s union strike leader Derek 'Red Robbo' Robinson to the Bullring, where they propped him up against the bronze bull.

Puzzled shoppers stopped to look. More than one commented it was probably a publicity stunt for Al Murray's Pub Landlord's latest tour. Joe didn't understand that, but he didn't care. He really couldn't see a summery Saturday afternoon in 2006. He heard the throaty patter of competing fruit sellers, with the smell of smoke and fried onions and the taste of Brew 11. And he saw a sepia-tinted scene from thirty years ago, when this was his Brum.

Liza Granville

LIZA GRANVILLE's novel, *Curing the Pig* ('a massively addictive and surreal black comedy' *Big Issue*) is published by Flame Books. Immanion are to publish two further novels, *The Crack of Doom* (2006) and *Until the Skies Fall* (2007).

Flower Power
Liza Granville

Having overgrown 1960s children as parents had caused much embarrassment to Tryphena Celestial Love-child Rainbow over the years.

As she saw it, life had been a humiliating experience, right from the word *zygote*. It was no secret that her conception, planned for the almond groves of Kathmandu, had apparently taken place in an old post office van stuck for thirty-six hours in the no-man's-land between Turkey and Iran while border guards indolently swatted bluebottles and philosophized over the lack of requisite documents. A mere thirty thousands rials, *Allah O Akbar*, might have changed the course of her life, but bribery, *man*, was out of the question. The pair were turned back, only to be stoned, or rather pelted with bones and overripe watermelons, the minute they recrossed the Turkish frontier by villagers who *knew* all Western women were harlots.

Six weeks later, the van died noisily on the European side of Istanbul and, since details of a motor vehicle appeared on their passports, it was impossible to leave the country without it. Tryphena's mother, morning-nauseous and desperate, finally traded her waist-length red hair an inch from the scalp in exchange for being smuggled into Greece in a consignment of carpets. Penniless and suffering from dysentery, they were repatriated from Belgrade and forswore foreign travel for all time.

Back in Britain, they opted for a simple life, in harmony with Mother Nature. Their families packed them off to a semi-derelict longhouse in deepest Devon, a gloomy place surrounded by Styx-black pines, set at an unmarked crossroads and already haunted by generations of regrets. They were promised enough capital to set up a cottage industry – both had dabbled in Art College ceramics – provided they suffered the compulsory twenty-minute register office ceremony.

The story, variously embellished, was trotted out at social gatherings with monotonous regularity to justify, Tryphena suspected, an existence lived festeringly close to the earth. She hated Nature. The energy of deep dark despair coursed through her veins and the subconscious longing for oblivion, planted before memory began, continued to wage war with her body's determination to survive. Obsessed by the idea of death, and yet terrified by the reality of it, anything that shattered life's saccharine monotony attracted her. Her first clear memory was of sitting in a meadow, slowly and carefully pulling all eight legs off a trapped spider while her mother waxed lyrical over the first cuckoo and gathered young *Urtica* tips to make a version of Samuel Pepys's nettle porridge. Tryphena's handiwork had been greeted with appalled silence and a swift slap, for which her mother profusely apologized. A diet of bedtime stories personifying insects followed, but Tryphena had already learned to conduct her experiments in secret. She relished that sadistic streak. Furtiveness was bred in her bones.

At school, she studied ancient history before she fully understood the mechanics of reproduction. She honestly believed that genetic material from the bellicose Medes and Persians had somehow been drawn from Iranian clay and ether to spark her embryo self. Even when interminable afternoons of Mendelism and sex education seemed to disprove her theory, she went on harbouring a belief in some psychic Middle Eastern connection because she felt so alien from her floating, doting, mutually dependent parents.

They were now quite elderly – in their mid-forties – still objecting vociferously to the Establishment; still wearing variants of the beads, loons and kaftans of their youth; still growing and smoking *weed*, and making foraging trips for magic mushrooms to the lower slopes of South Dartmoor. It was sheer fluke that Norn Pottery made money. Both professed to despise filthy lucre and spent little, driving around, barefoot, in a decrepit Morris Traveller held together with baler twine, and surviving on a macrobiotic diet of brown rice, more brown rice, and whatever ventured its head above the soil in the dank garden.

Tryphena grew up wiry and troubled. Her infant wails for attention – drowned by Pink Floyd at full volume – grew steadily louder and more raucous, but stopped abruptly with the realization that her parents were so wrapped up in each other that she might as well not be there. As she grew older, she saw herself as a mere fact of their existence. She craved strong colours, hot smells, movement, while the ancient house, earth-hued, dusty and damp, crammed with goblin shadows and roofed with mouldy thatch, felt like a living grave.

Puberty brought – bewilderment. She *beamed* hate.

Harmony and Peace refused to be shocked. Without ever really listening, they were so damned understanding that whatever rage-fuelled course Tryphena attempted to explore was fine with them. Nicotine-yellowed fingers didn't merit comment. The filthiest of language was merely an experiment in self-expression. No garment was so weird that Harmony didn't also try it for size. By the age of ~~thirteen,~~ both buttocks and her left ankle bore intricately vulgar tattoos. Later, she took body piercing to its innermost limits. A newspaper photograph of Tryphena, fourteen, mud-encrusted, naked and stoned at Glastonbury, was enlarged and framed for the dining room. Publicizing the early jettison of her virginity earned her dinner at a Plymouth health food restaurant. Harmony wore patchwork. Peace brought his own wine: a pungent 1989 elderflower champagne smelling of tomcat and secretly fortified with vodka. As the old car lurched and bucketed back up the A38, Tryphena crouched low, wishing herself invisible while her parents invented contemporary lyrics for Joan Baez protest songs. Halfway through a maudlin elegy for cows exterminated during the BSE scare, Harmony wept for the wickedness of the human race and the deliberate misinterpretation of Genesis 1: v.26 to justify eating their fellow creatures. Peace pulled over. They hugged and congratulated each other on their vegan purity.

Tryphena smiled into the darkness.

Next day she brought home two lambchops and half a kilo of pigs' liver. The smell of charred flesh brought her parents screaming from their kick-wheels. Scarlet-faced from prolonged retching but sure of their full attention, Tryphena announced that she had become a carnivore. The results were gratifying. Her mother wept. Her father cursed. Within a fortnight both Harmony and Peace wore the abstracted, non-comprehending faces Tryphena had observed on the parents of her friends.

She built on her success by developing an unhealthy obsession with the power of hard cash and threatened to take a degree in Business Studies. Her parents despaired. Actually, she had no interest in an academic future. Although she was not artistically gifted – in spite of having learned to throw pots at the age of four – she had decided to apply for a course in Visual Performance at the local Arts College, an institution which prided itself on its avant-garde reputation. With her sights firmly fixed on financial success, Tryphena had studied the shock value of certain Turner Prize winners and knew the college would provide her with the support and contacts she needed to replicate the drama of that moment in the kitchen, when all emotional hell had been let loose and for the very first time the focus had been entirely on her. One A Level and a portfolio constructed inside a lavatory pan won her a place. She cooked tofu and rice with dandelion leaves and marigold petals before producing the written offer. Again, her parents' reaction proved highly satisfactory. This time Peace wept with gratitude and her mother uttered orgasmic cries.

For most of the course Tryphena bided her time, quietly experimenting with the trimmings of death, animal bits and pieces – bones, particularly skulls, fur, teeth and feathers, a frog skin or two, rabbit tails, occasional wings. Moved by some instinct she hardly understood, for her first individual project, entitled *Talking About Women's Problems: Shhhhhh!*, Tryphena covered an entire studio floor with eggshells, which she had collected from local restaurants, bakeries and nursing homes. It had taken a month to amass such a quantity. They lay, pale green and six deep, sliming quietly onto the bare boards. The sulphurous stench coiled along corridors, fingering under doors, wafting through kitchen and refectory, sneaking past coughing, choking secretaries to linger in the complacent warmth of the Principal's office. A large audience was drawn to the haunt of this noxious Pied Piper. Violently crunching shells beneath her Doc Martens intensified the smell to the nth degree. Two students fainted. The bar opened early. Beyond a flat statement that it concerned *mis*-conception, of art, of ova, Tryphena refused to explain her piece and became flamboyantly aggressive when pressed.

The stage was set. Her fledgling reputation established, she next devised an installation (*Mute comme un Poisson*) centred on a large and very dead rainbow trout, stinking to high heaven and seething with maggots bought from a local fishing shop, among which she distributed tiny slips of acetate, each bearing a single letter. It was an exercise in accidental juxtapositions. Bizarre word combinations formed and re-formed as the maggots wriggled and tunnelled and waxed fat. This was so badly received that she delightedly moved on to exhibits of accident victims. Spring had come and the Devon lanes were thick with sacrificial victims. *The Quick and the Dead* featured advertising material for a new motorized offering from the Rover stable untastefully wrapped around half a dozen flattened hedgehogs. She laughed in the face of the assessor and scraped a bare pass. Only shock value was important now. When the remains of two cats, one ginger, the other a portly tabby, were arranged so that their mangled intestines spelled out *Catastrophe*, the cleaner contacted the local Cats Protection League. Their outraged reaction earned her a visit from the RSPCA and two lines in a London broadsheet courtesy of a freelance journalist.

For her penultimate show, *Unspeakable*, the first open to the public, she decided on risking an action-packed performance. A neighbour, who had seen her collecting feathers in the early months of the course, presented her with a mature cock pheasant, decidedly dead, but hardly marked. She thanked him prettily, hung it till it was well and truly high, and then bribed a fellow student with a motorbike to run across it in front of the audience. He agreed, but made the mistake of returning to inspect his handiwork, upon which he promptly threw up. Tryphena and the more robust of the onlookers responded with raucous cheers.

Harmony and Peace watched in stunned silence. Some of

the gore had splashed the drooping sleeves of Harmony's dress, a green velvet creation bought specially for the occasion. Glancing down, she saw that her husband's sandals were speckled with blood. His face was pale. His hair was stringy and grey. His hands were knotted and gnarled. Sudden terror washed over her, great waves threatening to engulf her, a melange of dark memories and realizations which boiled down to two simple facts: her daughter was a monstrous stranger, and *homo ludens* had ceased to exist – they were no longer the carefree innocents who laughed, celebrated and promised each other never to grow old. She ran from the building before the seventh wave could break.

In the silence of her room Harmony made a brave try at turning back the years, clipping off the white-streaked hair to within an inch of her scalp. It was full moon and the habitual agonizing stomach cramps accompanying the winding down of her internal clock knotted into her centre, drawing upwards, almost like birthing pains in reverse. Peace locked himself in the studio and threw pots until his hands seized up. In the morning Harmony, preparing to fettle, noticed how uterine they were, how fragile. Working methodically along the rows, she squeezed the life from each of them. It was three days before they could bring themselves to speak to each other. Nothing would ever be the same again.

Laughing inwardly, Tryphena professed not to notice anything amiss. She was already engrossed in planning her degree show, less than two months away. This was her launch into the art world, her big chance. Someone from the Arts Council always attended. Commissioning agents would be present. Whatever she produced had to be truly, deeply, madly shocking; so sickening that it would earn national condemnation.

Like so many others before her, she turned to myth and legend for inspiration. Something from the land of her spiritual birth would have been ideal, but since she envisaged drawing on the work of both Hirst and Whiteread she was forced to settle for Greece, focusing on the story of Pasiphaë.

Over Sunday breakfast she outlined her idea. She had recently viewed a video of a Dartington performance artist meticulously taking apart a grey suit and laying out the pieces on the floor of a large warehouse. She would do the same with a cow, scooping out its organs with a silver spoon to leave a cavity into which she could climb. It would take her three days, perhaps a little longer. She would have preferred to turn the creature inside out, but this required the guidance of a scientist, and Tryphena was not one to share her glory. The carcass would be purchased locally, from an old-fashioned farmer who butchered his own animals. This meant, she sniggered into the chill silence, that she could *pick her own* beast as it wandered around the buttercup meadows.

What did they think of *Pasiphaë Disremembered* as a title? No? She was stuck on this one. Anyone have any better ideas?

'Maybe,' said her mother, wearily getting up to make a herbal brew from the leaves and petals stored in one of the fifty or so stoneware jars on top of the dresser. Today she was wearing a jumble-sale cardigan over her flowered Indian dress, but shivered violently in spite of the bright June sunshine. Peace, who had aged ten years in as many weeks, mumbled some unintelligible expletive through a mouthful of organic muesli. Harmony poured boiling water into three mugs.

'Let's drink this. It might make everything clearer.'

Tryphena finished the pale gold, green-smelling liquid first. She had never really bothered to pursue that question of genes. Perhaps she should have done. In her own way,

Harmony was as ruthless as her daughter. Certainly, she knew when enough was enough. It was Harmony who'd ventured forth to break the stalemate all those years ago on the Turkish border while Peace lay sleeping. She could still smell the fetid air in that customs building; Tryphena's dark curls never let her forget it.

The Flower Power movement might have withered and died, but the power of flowers springs eternal. Considering the variety of plants growing in the Devon countryside, relatively few are poisonous to humans. But there are enough. Both sorts of hellebore can kill, so can cow-bane and columbine, the spindle tree, monkshood, baneberry, all species of buttercup, lily-of-the-valley, laburnum, fritillary, spurge, privet, dog's mercury, ivy, buckthorn, waterdrop hemlock, bryony, naked ladies, foxglove and, of course, deadly nightshade. All these, the self-styled Harmony had collected and preserved: her pact with Mother Nature meant she knew a lot more about the properties of flowers, seeds and leaves than was good for her. Nobody, least of all Harmony, had ever thought to question this malignant harvest.

For more than twenty years she'd borne her secret in silence, trying to make amends, sensing that there was yet time for dreadful retribution, but never expecting her journey to bring her back to no-man's-land. This one might be less tangible, but it was still a place of impasse, and one from which there was no other escape. At least the power to gauge when enough was enough hadn't deserted her.

Harmony drained her mug and reached for her sleeping husband's cold fingers, while all around them the smell of infused flowers lay sweet and potent on the warm air.

Neapolitan Ice
Liza Granville

With a more than usually jaundiced eye, Giuseppe Borelli assessed his party of tourists for tip potential. The coach was half empty, unusual for the Pompeii run, and what passengers there were consisted of a regular *fritto misto* of nationalities.

From long experience he knew the Japanese could safely be ignored. Raw fish, he thought scathingly; but treated courteously and presented with unlimited quantities of photographable material, they'd be adequately generous. One quick glance dismissed the three girls: two large green pears and an unripe peach, nothing there; nor from the stony-faced German, an unpalatable potato *gnoccho* if ever he saw one; his fellow countrymen were, almost without exception, burdened with deep pockets and short arms. As for the English couple, that rather depended on how well he could work the old Latin charm routine on the wife, a huge, quivering *zuppa inglese* of a woman. Naturally her husband, a shrivelled strand of *linguine*, didn't count.

As far as food and gratuities went, Giuseppe was an expert – his embonpoint told its own tale – and he'd been at this game so long he could calculate today's takings to the nearest centesimo. Borellis had been couriers of one sort or another for generations. Family legend claimed it had been a Borelli who'd carried certain packages from the apothecary for Lucrezia Borgia herself. In time, she'd destroyed him, of course, but luckily such treacherous, scheming women no longer existed. Giuseppe was proud of his profession: it was an honourable calling, the ultimate position of trust . . . not that he trusted anyone else.

Naturally, there'd been career disappointments. These days, opportunities were limited. For years only his position as tour guide had kept pasta and red wine on the table. Now, at last, he'd come into his own. Violent upheavals in certain neighbouring states – and lately somewhat further eastwards – had led to a steady flow of lucrative commissions; looted valuables were still being smuggled out via the Adriatic to an avid, blind-eyed world where nothing really ever changed. Most were small things: miniature art treasures, icons, jewellery, precious stones, things that could be stuffed into crevices and retrieved by surreptitious sleight of hand. Giuseppe approved of such simple, old-fashioned methods. His role was to smuggle the items aboard his vast person and convey them to dealers in Rome. He was the flavourless running water that baffled any hounds on the scent of such toothsome delicacies.

Today's consignment marked the pinnacle of his career: ice. It included one diamond reputedly rivalling the second cut of the Cullinan in size, hence worth an astronomical figure. Undoubtedly, these gems were already being sought but, entering the site via the Porta Marina, Giuseppe was unconcerned. Tonight he would celebrate at a proper *ristorante* instead of economizing at his regular *buco*. With his thoughts lingering over an elaborate imaginary menu, he led his party onto a grassy cobbled street, chomping through the script in his customary monotone.

'. . . and was buried under some six metres of volcanic

ash when Mount Vesuvius erupted in seventy-nine AD.'
Giuseppe glanced at his watch, noted they were five minutes
over schedule and quickened his pace. From the corner of
his eye he saw the Englishwoman's cavernous mouth open
and he flinched, resisting the impulse to duck and clap his
hands over his ears as her screech peaked.

'Harold! Harold! Come along. Keep up!'

Harold squeaked a faint reply. Giuseppe turned and saw
the little man scampering along twenty paces to the rear,
weighed down by his wife's impedimenta. *Mamma mia*, no
Italian man would permit himself to be so humiliated. Still
walking backwards, he let his eyes slide lazily past, searching for Andrej. And there he was, clicking his prayer beads
in the khaki shadow of the olive trees. Their eyes met,
whereupon Andrej gave an almost imperceptible nod and
slouched towards the trattoria.

Then Giuseppe caught his breath. Harold had stopped,
nose twitching – making him look more like an oversized
mouse than ever – as he stared with furtive longing towards
the trattoria's vine-shadowed courtyard, from where the
smell of garlic and sound of clinking glasses drifted entic-
ingly, and where pretty waitresses glided between customers, awarding warm smiles and cool drinks. A less astute
man might have felt compassion, but suspicion was the
predominant tool of Giuseppe's trade. What if the little
Englishman was not what he seemed? What if he was cun-
ningly sizing up Andrej?

Harold's wife had also noticed. A scream like an air-raid
siren ripped apart the heavy air. 'Ha-a-a-a-ROLD!'

'Yes, dear. Right away, dear.' Harold scampered after
her, his paws clutching and clawing at various bags and
spare garments. Giuseppe relaxed again. Halting in front
of a ruined building, he pointed out the mummified figures
cowering in one corner.

'Is this it?' asked someone.

'No!'

Giuseppe frowned. 'Forgotten for centuries,' he continued, raising his voice above the murmured conversation and ever-clicking cameras, 'it was rediscovered in seventeen forty-eight.'

'Ah, so? Seventeen forty-eight.'

'Approximately three-quarters of the ancient city has now been excavated, bringing to light many interesting and unknown facets of Roman –'

'Oh, Giuseppe.' In order to peer at his nametag, the peach came very close: so close that he could see the faint gold down on her arms and breathe in her sweet fruity fragrance; so close that his personal radar went on emergency alert. 'Giuseppe, are you quite, quite sure it's safe?'

'I said NO!' yelled the biggest pear, and clutched her forehead.

The insects had ferocious appetites at this time of year. Giuseppe gave a brief nod of sympathy before turning his attention back to the little peach who was, perhaps, riper than he'd first gauged. She tossed back a thick mane of blond curls. He managed a tight, professional smile. 'Safe, signorina?'

'Suella,' the vision chided him, fluttering sooty lashes, pouting extravagantly glossed lips and gesturing towards Vesuvius, looming over them and shimmering as it dozed in the intense heat. 'I expect you'll think I'm being *ever* so silly but, I mean, well, you said they had no warning . . . and . . . and it won't go and erupt on *us*, will it?'

She clasped her hands girlishly in front of her in such a way that her cleavage assumed even more dramatic proportions. Two of the bolder Japanese moved in to catch the moment on film. The German's gaze slid down to her haunches with the detached interest of a cattle breeder. An image of *sopa coada,* a deliciously rich soup containing morsels of fried bread and whole pigeon breasts, sprang to Giuseppe's mind and set him salivating. He tore his eyes away with some difficulty and calmed himself down by thinking of gristle.

'God Almighty!' The steatopygous pear – a Passacrassana, Giuseppe decided, plucked green and needing long, gentle cooking and much basting with honey and spices before it was fit to be devoured – stared contemptuously at Suella's pink shorts and plunging neckline. 'Females like you make a mockery of the ongoing struggle for sexual equality.' Her companion – the smaller, less developed pear, the flavourless Virgouleuse, mercifully rare – wriggled with embarrassment.

'Please don't start all that . . .'

The peach only smiled. 'Why don't you mind your own business?' she cooed, laying particular emphasis on the latter part of the sentence. 'Like right now?'

'Like *wrong* now,' mimicked the large pear. 'Stupid tart!'

Tarts? *Torta*? *Crostata*? Giuseppe, very partial to all kinds of pastries and *torta millefoglie* in particular, was fleetingly puzzled by the use of this word as an insult. Torn between irritation at losing the thread of his spiel and abject admiration of Suella's spectacular torso, it occurred to him that if the luscious peach was not with the two pears, then she must be travelling alone. Perhaps the celebratory dinner would be for two. He moistened his lips.

'Do not-a worry, signorina, you are in no danger here,' he gabbled, his fixed gaze and stentorian breathing contradicting the words. 'I, Giuseppe Borelli, give my word. Vesuvius, she last erupted in nineteen forty-four. Is only little, little steam now. Is very safe. Some of the finest grapes in all Italia are grown on its slopes.'

By exerting every last gram of willpower, Giuseppe

rounded up his charges and got them moving again. Choking white dust rose as they trudged on through the ruins. The German hunched over and began cursing softly to himself. Cameras clicked. The Englishwoman issued commands. Harold jumped to it. A few flies circled, but nothing else with any sense moved in the Campania landscape; even the ubiquitous gang of feral cats had slunk away to hide in the shade. At last they reached the Place and Giuseppe's heart began to pound with the familiar mixture of terror and excitement. He stopped, coughed delicately and smoothed his sleek moustache.

'We have before us Pompeii's ancient, er . . . brothel,' he murmured, 'with its unique pictorial tariff. Here the graffiti is of such an explicit nature that I regret only the gentlemen can be permitted to enter.'

This was the moment of power that made the job bearable. Other operators might have lowered their standards, but Giuseppe steadfastly abided by the guidelines issued to him in the early 1960s. Women were always outraged. Giuseppe thought of Mama's rod of iron and stood firm. The usual uproar ensued as the gist of his statement was translated and tossed backwards and forwards. The men looked at each other and grinned sheepishly, bound by a new sense of international brotherhood. Even Harold jubilantly drew back his lips, revealing tobacco-brown incisors.

Giuseppe stationed himself at the entrance. Five minutes more and he'd be a rich man. In spite of the heat, icy sweat trickled down his sides. Calm down, he told himself, relax. From this point onwards everything was straightforward. He knew exactly where the package would be hidden: just beneath a certain immoral and highly improbable act, to the left of one more probable, but equally indecent. He could find it blindfolded. Nobody would even notice. The men's attention would be held elsewhere. Generally, only women watched people watching things. And they were excluded.

Thirty seconds: that was all he needed. Thirty seconds.

So what was making him so anxious? Something was wrong. He could sense it. There was a terrible leaden feeling in his stomach: something like he'd experienced after being obliged to eat a double portion of Mama's *arrosta di vitello ubriacato* followed by far too much compensatory *zabaglione*.

He scanned the faces.

Without exception the Japanese stood, camera fingers poised, ready to shoot through the doorway. No obvious threat there, nor from his fellow Italians busily preening themselves. How about the three silly girls, looking daggers at each other – or Harold fidgeting with impatience, the wife glaring? Giuseppe dismissed them all. Instead, his gaze was drawn to the German, crimson-faced, pugnacious of jaw, his square head lowered and his pale eyes bulging ominously as he stared past everyone, towards the exit. This man could be a policeman – he looked angry enough, even his fists were clenched – and he seemed poised to leap into action. Giuseppe saw something that might have been panic flicker across his features, and his heart raced. Was the fellow waiting for reinforcements? The carefully visualized restaurant, its polished silver and immaculate napery, began to melt like so much *gelato*. With a supreme effort, Giuseppe got his fear under control. It was nothing. He was imagining things. Better get on with it. He ran his finger round his damp collar and comforted himself with thoughts of *ostriche alla veneziana* followed by *abbacchio*.

'Okay. Ladies. Is very nice temple on your right to look at.'

The large pear exploded. 'Like hell!'

Giuseppe jumped back in alarm. 'Signorina?'

'Temple? You've got to be kidding.' Towering over him, she jabbed a vicious finger into his chest. 'No way am I waiting outside while you lot get an eyeful of horny pictures.'

'Please, please, don't!' The small pear started blushing over every available inch of exposed skin. 'Not *now*.'

'For heaven's sake –' began the peach.

'Sharrup, both of you! Listen to me, Borelli.' Giuseppe stepped rapidly backwards as the large pear flourished the tour itinerary under his nose. 'I paid the same as everyone else. They see it. I see it. Simple as that. Bet there's nothing in there we can't see for real any night of the week on television. Now, show me *exactly* where it says women are excluded.'

'Leave it out,' hissed the peach. 'You're turning this into a dog's dinner.'

'Dog's dinner?' said Giuseppe, totally bewildered.

'She's just got this thing about equality, you see,' small pear explained to nobody in particular.

The large pear turned on her for the second time. 'Don't you DARE apologize for me!'

Small pear's lips began to tremble, whereupon the peach folded her arms over her chest and began tapping her foot.

The package had now been unguarded for seven minutes and thirty-three seconds. Anything could have happened. Giuseppe battened down a howl of rage and tried reverting to Italian charm.

'A thousand apologies, ladies, but is the custom . . .' He did his best but the charm had worked better twenty years ago and several stone lighter. Only the Englishwoman succumbed. She simpered. Harold watched, fascinated. The large pear was not impressed.

'Don't give me that crap.'

'Oh, dear.' Small pear wrung her fingers. 'I suppose you

can't blame her really. Women still aren't treated as equals, are they?'

Harold opened his mouth, caught his wife's eye and closed it again.

'I should have known better than to come on this jaunt with you two,' snapped the peach, suddenly anything but vacuous and sounding so like Mama that Giuseppe jumped. Catching his eye, she immediately turned coy. 'Go ahead, boys! I don't have any complaints about equality. But then, I enjoy being a woman.' She smiled towards the large pear. 'And *I'm* not a man-hater.'

Large pear shot her a look of pure loathing. 'I'll bet. Shouldn't think love or hate comes into it, but I bet cash does. By the look of you, I should imagine you feel completely at home here.'

Small pear gasped. The peach frowned and there followed a moment of silence as she appeared to wrestle with the implications of those words. Then her eyes narrowed. Her fingers curved into red-tipped talons. Giuseppe quickly placed himself between them.

'Ladies! Ladies! Can we please continue?' He mopped at his forehead. *Mamma mia!* What a nightmare.

'Well?' demanded the large pear.

'Is not written, Signorina.' He spread his hands. He favoured her with a Latin shrug. 'Is *bordello*. Is just not suitable for ladies.'

'Ladies, my arse! Haven't I made myself clear? Unless you can show me something, some notice, sign, anything, stating that women are excluded, I'm going inside.' She seemed to expand before his eyes. 'Try and stop me.'

'Signorina –'

'Bloody backward race, the Italians.'

'Signorina!' Giuseppe glared at her, drawing himself up to his full five foot two and a half inches. 'We Italians brought the world civilization – the baths, the pasta, the ice cream.'

'She doesn't mean to be rude,' gabbled the small pear. 'I expect she's overtired. Travelling. The heat . . .'

'Of course.' Recovering quickly, Giuseppe attempted a mild joke. 'Let us just say, when in Naples do as the Neapolitans do.' The Japanese produced polite smiles on cue. Giuseppe darted a quick glance into the brothel's dusty interior. There wasn't another proper entrance, but there were window openings. What if someone beat him to it? He suddenly noticed the German edging around the side of the building and brought him to heel with a sharp, 'Signor!'

'Stuff that!' Large pear hadn't finished. 'I paid to look round Pompeii and look round I damn well will.'

'Can't we just get this over with?' The small pear was examining her sensibly shod feet so intently that her words were muffled. Her shoulders shook. In happier circumstances Giuseppe would have thought the poor girl was choking back laughter.

The Englishwoman sniffed. She tightened her cardigan more securely around her well-bolstered front. 'All I can say is, no decent woman would want to set eyes on such filth.'

'Silly cow.' Large pear treated her to a John Wayne sneer. 'It's so-called *decent* women who've allowed male chauvinist pigs to get away with murder for centuries.'

'Are you going to let her speak to me like that, Harold?'

Harold trembled. A small whimper emerged.

'It's you that's the silly cow,' snapped the peach. 'Can't leave it alone, can you? You've lost sight of the real objective. Think of the bread.'

Bread? Giuseppe scratched his head.

'Money equals power,' she continued, apparently apropos of nothing, 'and power is what women are really short of.'

'Who the hell d'you think you're talking to?' demanded

the large pear, giving the peach such a sharp jab in the solar plexus that it overbalanced her and sent her staggering into Giuseppe's arms. Giuseppe looked down at the girl's rounded bosom and was irresistibly reminded of generous scoops of apricot *gelato*. His jowls quivered. It took him a whole minute to recover himself. He was still setting the poor girl on her feet, dusting imaginary dust off her front, when the large pear uttered a very rude, and not altogether inappropriate word, and strode determinedly into the brothel ruins.

'NO!' Giuseppe was about to scuttle after her, but found himself impeded by the peach, still clinging tightly to his arm, her eyes brimming with tears. In that same moment he noticed the German again attempting to sneak away, and that little rat, Harold, scuttling after the large pear. It was essential to keep every member of the party within sight. 'You come-a back here!' he bawled at them both. Accustomed to obeying instructions, Harold froze. His wife pursed her lips in disapproval as the small pear sank to the ground laughing hysterically and, en masse, the Japanese tittered uncomprehendingly behind their hands. With some difficulty, Giuseppe shook off the clinging peach, threw up his hands and dived into the brothel. All of the men – with the exception of the German, who took the opportunity to race towards the toilet – and some of the women followed him. The Englishwoman hovered in the doorway pretending not to look. The Italians lit cigarettes and adopted supercilious expressions.

Hands stuffed into her pockets, the large pear was standing in the middle of the floor staring up at the walls. 'Is this it? Is *this* what all the fuss was about? I've seen raunchier on a New York subway. What a disappointment.' With a look of disdain she marched back outside.

Giuseppe breathed a sigh of relief. He edged towards a

certain depiction of human interaction that he'd memorized by means of visualizing *lingua in gelatina* – one of his favourite cold dishes – and casually ran his hand along the wall, feeling for the crevice. There was no package. Nothing. He looked high, he looked low, he fingered the stones, seeking out the smallest orifice, he minutely examined representations of every variation of the sexual act known to Roman man, men, woman and women. Nothing.

Two minutes later, he emerged ashen-faced and empty-handed to find that all three girls had vanished. The wine cleared: like a kid led to the slaughter, he, Giuseppe Borelli, had been set up. His goose was cooked. The chips were down. The fat was in the fire. His reputation had been shredded. Alas, tonight, tomorrow and all the days to come he would have to sing for his supper. It was left to the Japanese tourists to photograph the last of the Borelli line banging his head against the walls of a Pompeii cathouse, shrieking gross imprecations about womankind, a female called Lucrezia and also, for some inexplicable reason, reciting the many and varied indigestible properties of peaches and pears.

Laurence Inman

LAURENCE INMAN used to hold lots of opinions, but in the course of a long and eventful life has managed to whittle them down to one. It's this: there is exactly the right amount of happiness in the world and any more would just spoil things.

Danny the Bastard

Laurence Inman

Danny the Bastard was so called for three good reasons.

First, his name was Danny.

Second, he was a bastard.

Lastly (it always gave him a flutter of self-congratulation to consider this), he rose to local prominence in his chosen profession at a time (the mid-1970s) when it was advantageous, if not de rigueur, to adopt a sobriquet which encapsulated, in strong and direct terms, one's approach, both practically and philosophically, to one's duties and responsibilities. It was, in fact, an indispensable aspect of Public Relations.

His professional christening (as it were) also coincided with that time when it seemed inconceivable not to adopt the middle name *the*.

Danny was always pleased he had made his name before the emergence of the rather regrettable fashions in nomenclature which followed that brilliant, unsurpassed decade.

Danny's associates, Unpredictable Den and Morose Jeremy, were, of course, unsullied products of this later time, as were also, in their own way, Peter Nosh and Grim Brian. Things progress, Danny knew, but even so, the current trends (hip-pop, garage, or whatever the fuck it was called), which gave birth to oddities like Ark-Symbolic and Fang-Sang-Do-It, and which would have rendered him down to D/Bast or some such, dismayed him.

Names date you. When this generation becomes Grandma Kylie and Granddad Tyler they'll see this. But not before, thought Danny bitterly. Because they can't see further than the ends of their snooker cues. If they ever played snooker. Or had even heard of it. They can't appreciate the wider picture, place their small doings in the broad sweep of historical necessity. They are, in short, thick. Yes. Docile, willing consumers of whatever crap is put on their plate. Drug – in all fucking likelihood – addled.

These musings and mutterings were the staple fare of the chaps' afternoon conversations in the back room at Knuckles. If the truth were told, they also made up most of the neurological traffic in Danny's mind these days. He was, he knew, beginning to sound like the idea he had built up of his dad. 'Look at the state of him!' and 'Have you seen what time of night it is!' were typical of the remarks his dad might have made as he stumbled into late middle age, if he hadn't died after having been stitched up and then banged up in various places around the country.

Danny was now older than his dad had been when he died. He was now more than twice as old as his dad had been on D-Day.

Visions of his dad's exploits in Normandy still flickered on the cinema screen of Danny's imagination.

'All the others landed on D-Day, son, but I waded ashore alone from my midget sub three days earlier, on A-Day.'

From there he had, virtually single-handedly, demolished Pegasus Bridge, blown up railway tracks, pulled down telephone lines, organized the Resistance into passably good fighting units and personally led them in assaults on the key defensive positions overlooking the beaches.

'By the time the rest of the army arrived it was as good as finished, son. I tried to tell Churchill. Don't bother, I said, but he said the Americans expected a big show, so a big show they had to have. All that stuff on the so-called sixth of June was just for the cameras.'

He was called the Lion of Normandy. Before that he'd been called the Lion of the Western Desert. 'They had a comic strip about me in *The Eagle*. "The Lion of Normandy!" They ran the same one, more or less, in *The Lion*, but in that I was called "The Eagle of Normandy".' He would, he said, show Danny the carefully stored copies of these papers, but they were in Granddad's attic and they never visited him because, his dad said, he had only won the Battle of the Somme, an altogether less momentous event, and it just wouldn't do for him to be seen round there.

For his services on A-Day, Dad was awarded the Victoria Cross *and* the Croix de Guerre *and* the Iron Cross with oak leaves, a unique achievement. 'The Germans gave me the Iron Cross as a bribe to stay at home. I promised I would and the idiots believed me!'

'Can I see your medals, Dad?'

'When we go and see your granddad, son.'

His mom's version of those days was at some variance with his dad's.

According to her he had spent the entire war either in gaol or dodging the authorities. Danny had learnt from bitter experience in Life, in Philosophy and in courtrooms, that the truth was almost always at the exact midpoint between two opposing fictions, so he was quite happy to accept that, in reality, his dad had landed on D-Day like everybody else, or at best had floated to earth on C-Day with a special paratroop unit, and that he'd only won the Victoria Cross.

Whatever. And here he was, the years having spun past him, and he'd done nothing.

It worried him. Time was really beginning to mean it. When he was a kid, it was different. Next year was unimaginably distant. Summers stretched on for two summers. Now Christmas comes round every ten weeks or so. Another Olympics. Another World Cup. Time, numbers themselves, which, as Bertrand Russell pointed out, have a 'Pythagorean power holding sway above the flux', were in a state of warping and shrinking. A boulder was bounding down the hill; Danny couldn't see it missing him.

He tried to keep his broodings hidden from the others; it wouldn't do to reveal such things to them. They were a loyal bunch: strong and steady and willing to follow any orders if they thought it would help to keep things together, and not just for their own personal profit or self-aggrandizement either. Such bonding can only be found in one place. Danny hated clichés, but it was true: they were one big happy extended kinship network.

It was Saturday afternoon. Another Saturday afternoon. Danny and the boys (Unpredictable, Grim, Morose and Peter) were in the back. Some of the younger chaps had gone to the Villa, some to the other place to watch whatever it was they did down there. Danny had long since seen through the spurious emotional manipulations of football. For a time he used to amuse himself at Antoninus, the bookie two doors down, but even this had begun to pale; if he won, so what? If he lost, it came back to him sooner or later. Usually sooner.

Numbers. It was always numbers.

'Cheer up, Dan,' said Grim. 'It might never happen!'

Danny looked up briefly. 'If I'd hit all the fucking stupid twats,' he said, 'who'd ever said that to me, the hospitals would have to close.'

In the silence that followed, the others glanced warily at each other, one or two of them trying to work out Danny's words to their semiotic and imaginative conclusion.

They all knew what was worrying him. There was another association (they called themselves a 'crew') on the other side of town. They too had their leadership hierarchy, almost identical in construction and composition to their own. Their deputy, the equivalent of Unpredictable, was called T;Shit. They used to think he was called T'Shit, as in the northern idiom: *Tha dog's dropped t'shit in t'street*. The misunderstanding had been, at length and with some discomfort, resolved to both sides' satisfaction only a few months previously. A gnat's memory-length.

The leader of this 'crew' didn't have a conventional name, but a symbol. It was this:

Danny and the boys had no way of interpreting this. Where were the shared cultural concatenations which would enable them to start making sense of it? Nowhere, that's where. In an icy silence. They didn't even know how to pronounce it. When they talked about this leader-person they had to utter a kind of indeterminate *Nyerr* and so that became his name. What else could they do?

Grim Brian plucked up the courage to break the silence. 'Is it Nyerr, Dan?'

Danny shrugged and continued to stare into his cup of Earl Grey.

The others were encouraged. They all wanted to say, 'We'll go and kill him for you, Dan!' But of course it wasn't that simple. Only Danny could make that kind of decision.

Peter spoke next. 'We still don't know the facts, Dan. It could have been a slip of the tongue.'

Danny looked up wearily. 'Peter, we've been through all that. Haven't we? Haven't we?'

'Yes Dan.'

'Yes Dan. And what did we decide?'

'That we'd give it a week . . .'

'Danny can't hear you!'

'That we'd give it a week.' Peter went on more loudly, 'And if we hadn't heard either a retraction, or an explanation, or that Nyerr had disciplined T;Shit to our satisfaction for his gross transgression, then a state of unpleasantness would obtain between us.'

Peter breathed with relief, glad that he'd been able to remember the exact wording of the resolution.

Danny exploded. 'It's all fucking words!' he screamed.

The others couldn't help flinching slightly.

'He said it! He said it! They all heard! He heard, that fucking Nyerr, and he said nothing about it.'

'Dan . . .' Morose began.

'Oh, *you*'ve fucking woken up at last, have you?'

Morose sank back into his chair.

'Don't tell me it was a slip of the fucking tongue. He said it. That shit T;Shit said, when the others had been discussing Danny the Bastard, with all the proper respect, as far as we know, he had made a contribution to the conversation, during which he decided to refer to me as Danny that Bastard. Danny *that* Bastard. And that turd Nyerr was there listening, and what did he do? Eh? What did he say?'

The others looked intent and baffled.

'Nothing, that's what! Fuck all! He just stood there. And laughed, probably!'

'We don't know that, Dan,' at least two of them chimed in, hopefully.

'I know it! I know it!' screamed Danny.

They all jerked back. They had never seen him this upset.

'Don't you think I know how it goes, after all this time? Eh? Eh?'

He suddenly stopped and stared ahead. He knew, if anybody did, how it went and how it would go. 'Never give them an inch, son,' his dad had always said. But an inch of what? And who were *they*?

'Leave me alone for a bit, boys. I didn't mean to shout at you. It's not your fault.'

They tumbled out together.

Words, thought Danny, words! Again and again, it came to the same thing. This word, this apparently tiny substitution, *that* for *the*, was the microscopic cancerous cell which would multiply and swell every time it was repeated. It was an atom of icy water in the bottom brick of the wall surrounding Danny's very existence. Frost in a brick expands and splinters, the fabric crumbles like pastry, the wall is weakened and eventually will fall.

If only Nyerr hadn't heard! Things would have been so simple! T;Shit would have been dealt with by someone of similar rank, Unpredictable probably, although it could have provided a good opportunity to give one of the younger lads an outing, that new fellow from Wolverhampton, Custard Paperweight or whatever the fuck he'd decided to call himself, nice kid, could go far with the right encouragement . . .

But what was the point of thinking about what *could* have happened? The situation was what it was, and would have to be dealt with on that basis. Nyerr had not stamped on T;Shit for calling Danny *that* . . . THAT Bastard. It was that *that* that made the future inevitable.

*

It came very suddenly, as both of them knew it would. With such people there are no childish threats, no arranged meetings, no risk of escalation. How could things escalate from this? But enough of causality.

They each found themselves in the same place: Material, at the back of Broad Street. Glances were exchanged. Whisperings and noddings and assured smiles were passed around between members of the separate groups. Inches were neither given nor lent; nor would they ever be: that was clear.

They circled each other a couple of times. Nyerr was excellent at this bit. Like a dancer. Then he caught Danny, once. Danny immediately hit back, twice. Nyerr hit back four times. Danny replied eight times. Nyerr sixteen times . . .

Was it then, as their eyes registered recognition of an emerging theme, that the mysterious engine of folklore was already elaborating a name for this event? The Great Geometric Progression Fight.

They went on, in seconds getting up to five hundred and twelve.

That was Danny. Now it was Nyerr's turn. But he had to get clever, didn't he? He had to get smart. He went $4n + 10$, where n was the number Danny had done. So instead of 1024 he jumped straight to 2058.

Danny thought hard and fast. What could he do? Follow him? Think of his own formula? Go back to a simple $2n$?

He thought too long. In a millisecond Nyerr adopted $6n + 40$, and would probably have gone on to develop even more surprising and original variations.

Game over.

Danny sank to the floor.

What flashed through his mind in those seconds? Anger? Regret? Not at all. There were no bitter thoughts, only the calm acceptance we all must face as our time gathers and speeds through its final few moments, as it races, as it accelerates towards the immovable destination. He had always known this. But only, as it turned out, theoretically. He had failed to recognize the specific context of his own destiny: the who, the where, the why.

Doesn't everybody? The new men with their new names and their new ways of seeing things are forever nudging you forwards, out of the way.

In the back room at Knuckles they put up a little plaque. It read simply:

OF YOUR CHARITY, PRAY FOR THE REPOSE
OF THE SOUL OF DANNY THE BASTARD

A year later Knuckles became Thumbs. The new owners took down the plaque. But not before somebody had scrawled out *the* and written *what a*.

New Departures
Laurence Inman

'I came into teaching for two good reasons: July and August.'

The man-with-four-chins who said this rocked and guffawed in his chair.

'Her, her, her-herrrr-her-her,' he went on, showing the shreds of his salad bap.

Several other people in the staff room (the knitting-woman, the crossword-man, the fruit-woman, the big-hairy-bloke-in-shorts, the old-git-in-glasses and the eager-to-please-student) smirked in response.

Tim Lazenby, looking at them all from his tatty armchair in the corner, almost smirked too. He always almost-smirked when he heard this joke. In fact, his response had hardly altered since the first time he'd heard it, in some similar staff room in Bradford. Or was it Huddersfield? No: definitely Bradford. Since then, his 'career' as a supply teacher had sent him meandering across the country: after Bradford, *then* there was Huddersfield and then Manchester, Wolverhampton, back to Manchester, then Exeter, London (ghastly!), Exeter again, Bristol, Newbury (very nice), London (ghastlier!), Worcester, Leicester, Wolverhampton (not improved), and now Birmingham. In all these places he'd dutifully almost-smirked at this joke, and many others.

Laurence Inman

Supply work suited him down to the ground. He liked being on the move. He loved settling in new towns, waking up in new flats, getting to know new pubs, new shops and new people. Occasionally he got to know new people very well. And there was the lovely surge of self-satisfaction and pride he got from being welcomed in to rescue people from a hellish situation. Rather like how a fireman must feel, he often thought, when he arrives at a scene of exploding chaos and calmly begins to unroll his hose. Most of the time he was sent to replace teachers who were said to be 'feeling the strain' or 'under a bit of pressure'.

The kids were a little more direct: 'Our last English teacher sat in the stock cupboard and tried to teach us from there.'

'Our last English teacher thought he was John the Baptist and Fatty Edgington in 11Y was Jesus.' (That one was surprisingly common.)

These were the colourful accounts. Others were less so: 'Our last English teacher went mad. Are you mad, sir? We can send you mad if you like, sir. Would you like that, sir? Eh? Eh? Eh?' And they could, he knew.

So it was always an exquisite pleasure when, after a few days or weeks, his work there finished, he savoured the special joy of strolling down the drive, thinking, *I never have to go back there!*

The job itself was a doddle, because he was spared all the things which ordinary teachers had to endure, those little things which bring on 'the odd bit of strain' or 'a spell of feeling under the weather'. Supply teachers have no real responsibility, no absurd expectations to live up to, no meaningless reports to write, no arse-clenching Parents' Evenings to sit through. Best of all, the money was excellent. And it would never end. The way the education system was going, schools would be run only by fresh, pink young

88

NQTs and world-weary supply staff. The rest would be on sick leave or trying to get early retirement – before joining the supply lists. It was happening already.

After ten years he was beginning to notice something else: all the schools and all the people in them were the same. There was always a four-chinned-man and he always made the July-August joke. There was always a terrified student, always a woman who ate nothing but fruit from a Tupperware box, always a thuggish Games teacher, always a Mr Bitter-and-Disenchanted and always, *always* a man in his late twenties swollen with unquenchable ambition.

Tim often thought wistfully of how he used to be that man, until Cathy came to her senses and ran off with the man who delivered their organic vegetables.

Their marriage had been the usual catastrophe: each of them had married the person they thought the other was, or should have been. Then each had tried to become the person they thought the other had thought they had married.

So that the couple everyone knew as Cathy-and-Tim were really *pretend*-Cathy and *pretend*-Tim . . . Then the pretend-people tried to adjust to what they thought the other pretend-person expected and/or wanted . . . So each of them became a pretend-pretend-person . . .

It isn't easy living in a story-within-a-story-within-a-story.

Cathy had been a teacher as well. She was a natural teacher. Children liked her. She smiled at them and listened to what they had to say. They smiled at her, easily and naturally. Lazenby thought he could manage all that. It didn't seem very difficult. Two things dispelled any doubts he might have had: July and August.

So, equipped with a very ordinary degree in English, he was content to see the rest of his life unfolding in a repeating series of ten-second film-loops. We are all tempted into dreams, especially in the bright dawn of youth. The new English teacher is presented with a bewildering array of fantasies. Of course, most choose Mr Chips. They see themselves growing old (but retaining a youthful twinkle), working in some ancient pile built of biscuit-coloured Cotswold stone. Through their study window they can hear reedy shouts from players in an eternal game of cricket. Beyond the rustling elms and lush meadows a river glitters in the middle distance. Spirited boys with names like Winthrop Minimus sit bright-eyed, soaking up their master's nuggets of knowledge and wisdom. They are loved and respected by generations of Winthrops, stretching into the future . . .

But this wouldn't do for Lazenby. No, he would work in a grainy monochrome school in the North. He would be like Colin Welland in *Kes*, only better looking. The kids would scoff at him, but he would win them over by sheer force of personality, enthusiasm for Literature and some feat of physical bravery, like rescuing one of their dads from a blazing pigeon shed. In the end they would, he imagined, come striding up to him after a lesson and say, 'By 'eck, sir, that quadruple period on Modernist Poetry between t'wars just flew by! Ah couldn't believe it when t'bell went! That T. S. Eliot – ah thought he were a right tight-arsed ponce at first, but he were some poet, him!' They would go on to become writers themselves. He would appear, beaming and modest, on *This Is Your Life* and eventually sit back in some pipe-smoke-wreathed, book-lined study, gazing out on the soft summer afternoon and the playing fiel . . . slagheaps.

But it was impossible. Teaching was, as Sam Johnson found before him, 'a complicated misery'. He became irritated by kids and their childish ways. Then teachers, with their adult ways, began to irritate him even more. Finally, he began to irritate himself. He learnt that self-disgust is the most relentless and destructive of emotions. He knew he should be somewhere else, and longed to be there, but he lacked the will to take the first step.

It was better now. He could put everything in its proper place on the ladder of importance. He could see that all of us have a slot in life, into which we will slide smoothly, once we have found it and if we are lucky enough to find it in time. This applied to everything: relationships, interests, jobs. That's why staff rooms everywhere contain the same people. They *have* to be there. It's their place. They think they chose that career, but no: it chose them.

The great trick was to find the other, proper place, the cosy little nest worn to just your shape, before it was too late. Seen in this light, Cathy's departure, and all life's jolts and disappointments, made perfect sense. She was not going to get to her real destination on the track she was riding, so she had to change trains. And that in turn meant *he* had to get off too, and have a cup of tea in the rather shabby cafeteria on platform five, where he could think what to do next. Should he get another train, or leave the station and find a bus?

These thoughts occupied him as the staff room emptied and the regular teachers trudged off to face afternoon registration, something else Tim was always spared. In fact, he didn't have a class at all. He was free until the last double of the day, *Macbeth* with Year 11. Easy peasy. Plenty of time to finish the crossword. Or even have a kip.

The deputy head, a fussy man, expert at looking stressed and put-upon (they all were), suddenly appeared. His name, as far as Lazenby knew, was Mobbing.

'Ah Mr Lazenby! The very man! Have you got a minute?'

Tim had had no time to cover his lap with books to be marked.

'Yes, I think so.'

'Good. Could we go to my office for a little chat?'

'Very probably.'

Mobbing looked at him doubtfully for a moment, then shrugged. Other people's senses of humour were obviously their own affair. They hurried off to his office.

'I had a rather unsettling telephone call this morning,' he began.

He leant back to survey the effect of this remark. He had clearly, thought Lazenby, read that story by P. G. Wodehouse in which one of the toffs in the Drones' Club thinks it a great wheeze to sit down next to perfect strangers in Hyde Park and whisper: 'I know everything!'

'Oh yes?'

'Yes.'

'Yes?'

'Yes.'

We used up this conversational line two yesses ago, thought Lazenby.

'And?' he said, for a change.

'And what? Oh yes,' said Mobbing.

He's very good, thought Lazenby. His *distrait* Mr Chips was one of the best he'd seen.

There was another blank silence. Brilliant, Lazenby allowed, but it was time to get to the point.

'Unsettling call . . .' he prompted.

'Oh yes. Yes, indeed. As you may know, Mr Turnbull is retiring at the end of the term.'

'Is he?'

'Yes. I thought everyone knew.'

'Well, I don't. I don't even know who Mr Turnbull is.'

'He's the Head.'

'Oh well, that explains it.'

'Yes, I know he's a rather remote figure.'

Remote? Lazenby thought he couldn't be more remote if he lived in Tibet. Not only had he never heard the name mentioned, he had, in his two months at the school, never even heard a single reference to the Head, not once.

'Anyway,' Mobbing went on, 'he has to be replaced.'

'If you say so.'

'I know what you're thinking. Why doesn't he apply for the job himself? Good question. Very good question. Well, I'm up for a headship somewhere else. I'm very confident. And we've been inundated with applications. This is bound to be the case with a school of this calibre. You should have seen the competition I had to fight off for my job. And it's not just senior management posts. Even the caretaker's position . . .'

While Mobbing was saying all this, Lazenby tried to calculate the exact number of days he'd been alive. 'Bloody leap years!' he whispered.

Mobbing looked, but said nothing.

'The thing is,' he went on warily, 'we've had one application in particular. Bloke called Almond. References make him sound like a cross between Bertrand Russell and Ghandi. Head and shoulders above the rest.'

'Sounds like he's the one,' said Lazenby.

'Sounds like it. Yes . . .'

Both of them knew, of course, that the worst teachers got the best references. It was a good way for schools to offload useless staff, get them promoted way beyond their competence so they could really mess things up, collapse under the pressure, get retirement, go on the supply list.

'Then this morning I had this call . . .'

'Oh yes, you said.'

'Asked to speak to me personally. A woman. Spoke breathlessly, as if she was afraid she'd be caught any moment. She was from Almond's school. In Wolverhampton.

Said we were about to make a big mistake. Called him an incompetent monster. That was the most charitable thing she called him.'

'Do you think it's a case of personal animus?' Lazenby ventured.

'Eh?'

'A grudge. You know what teachers are like.'

'It's possible, I suppose.'

'So you just cross him off the list.'

'Yes. The thing is, though, suppose he really is the genuine thing?'

'A Philosopher-King of Education, sent among us lesser beings to show us the True Path to Pedagogic Righteousness?'

Mobbing eyed him suspiciously. 'I wouldn't quite put it like that.'

'What you want is to talk to other members of staff there, find what the truth is about this Almond.'

'That may be one way. But suppose they don't want to talk? I mean, if he's as bad as this woman says, why should they tell us? They'll want rid of him, won't they? No, we have to find a way of getting to the unvarnished truth.'

We? What does he mean, *we*? 'Why don't you,' said Lazenby, entering into the spirit of things, 'send a little group of staff, disguised as window cleaners or photocopier repairmen? They could pick up all the gossip, the genuine truth, in less than a day.'

'I've got a much better idea.'

'What's that?' said Lazenby, already fearing the answer.

'We send you.'

'Me?'

'It'll be easy for you. You've worked on supply for that authority before, haven't you?'

'Yeees . . .'

'And the situation there, well it's as bad as here. You're certain to be able to specify any school you want to work in.'

'Probably.'

'And we'll pay your salary here while you do it. You'll be earning double.'

'Plus expenses?'

'If we must.'

'Done.'

And it *was* done. Very easily. He called the Wolverhampton education office. 'Yes, of course, Mr Lazenby. Glad you want to rejoin us. Dog Lane Comp? Sure. Shouldn't say this, probably, but they always need cover there. Just report to the deputy, Mr –'

'Almond.'

'That's right. You obviously know the place.'

Of course I do, he could have said, they're all identical.

And it went entirely to plan. He met Almond, a man for whom, at first sight, the words *weasel* and *nondescript* might have been invented. But he soon learnt there was more to Mr Almond than that. 'Incompetent monster' didn't do him justice. Oh no. He listened as the head of English revealed how Almond had discussed with him the possibility of 'reprocessing' the A-grade students' coursework over and over each year. 'It's foolproof,' he was reported to have said. 'The idiots post the bloody evidence back to us every September!' He recoiled as tales unfolded of Almond's financial chicanery, allotting precious resources to his own private projects, money which was never seen again. He sat transfixed as a woman (Mrs Phone Call?) hissed her sullen hatred of Almond in his ear: 'Do you know what that drunken pervert said to me at the Christmas so-called party? He said, he said, "You've got a lovely face, Anne. Do you know what would improve it?" Like an idiot I said,

"What?" And he said, "Seeing my balls on your chin." I was nearly sick. And his wife was only on the other side of the room!'

By the end of the week he had heard enough.

It was, Lazenby reflected, a sorry saga of moral degeneracy, devious embezzlement, vindictive double-dealing and alcohol-fuelled lechery. Only a madman would put such a person in charge of a whelk stall, let alone one of the second city's leading educational establishments.

He felt he'd done a good week's work. Mobbing would be delighted.

As he approached Almond's office on Friday afternoon, to bid him farewell before departing, whistling, from Dog Lane Comp, never to return, Lazenby heard the sound of sobbing. He leant closer to the door. There could be no mistake. Someone was in there, blubbing and whining in distress.

What was the little turd up to now? Threatening a probationer with some trumped-up misdemeanour if they didn't comply with one of his depraved suggestions?

Lazenby flung open the door.

Inside, Almond sat alone, crumpled at his desk, weeping like a child.

It was an appalling sight. Tears and snot mingled to form a glutinous pool on his desk.

'Mr Almond!' Lazenby said.

'Shut the door! Shut the door!'

In the compressed tension of that room, nothing broke the silence for some minutes but the snifflings and snortings from Almond's nose.

'Come on,' said Lazenby at last, his innate sympathy for his fellow edging aside the feelings of revulsion he had built up about the man. 'It can't be that bad.'

'It's worse,' Almond slubbered.

'Do you want to talk about it?'

Lazenby fully expected to hear some confession to a crime which would carry a minimum of five years; conspiracy to commit GBH, or sex with a Year 11 pupil at the very least.

'I hate this job!' Almond exploded. 'I've always hated it. I can't think why I ever thought I'd like it. Well, I can, actually.'

'July and August?'

Almond gave Lazenby a cold glance.

'I'm up for a headship, you know. I'll probably get it as well. I get brilliant references. Always have. Everywhere I've been. You know why? They can't wait to get rid of me. It's been the same all my career. I'm not an evil man, but this job makes me do and say the most terrible things. A headship! I'm dreading it. But I can't back out. She won't let me –'

'She?'

'My wife. She has to keep pushing me all the time. Her three airhead brothers are all successful businessmen . . . houses in the country, holiday homes abroad, big cars with personalized number plates – you know what I mean. And she's the poor relation, because she's married to me! That's why I've got to become a head. To make her feel better when she meets up with her brothers and their appalling wives and their fat kids once in a blue moon. I can't take it any more!'

Lazenby leant across the desk and, for once in his life, spoke the absolute and complete truth as he saw it. 'You're living in the wrong story.'

'Eh?'

'At the moment you're living in a particularly bleak story written by Chekhov. It's not for you. You want to be living in a story written by P. G. Wodehouse.'

'What are you talking about?'

'Look at me. I'm living in a Wodehouse story and I haven't got a care in the world. Nothing here is serious. Everything there,' he said, pointing to Almond's head, 'is deadly serious. Leave there and come here.'

'I still don't –'

'I am not what I seem.'

And Lazenby told him why he was really there.

II

And that is how it began. The business. The lovely thing which started to occupy their every waking minute, which expanded and diversified and grew its own personality (until the inevitable happened).

They would provide a unique service to schools looking for new senior teachers. They would root out and deliver the truth. In a field where mendacity traditionally rules supreme, where lies were positively encouraged, they would dig and mine and ferret until they lifted, pure and glinting, the diamond of veracity into the pellucid light of a spring dawn.

The first job they struggled with, at their first meeting at Almond's cluttered house with his kids screaming as they ran round the room, was to think of a name.

Almond's idea – *SchoolSnoop: Get The Dirt On Your Prospective New Head Before They Get Dumped On You!* – convinced Lazenby that perhaps his true abilities lay in the area of administration rather than creativity. They adopted instead *New Departures – School Staffing Solutions*, which Lazenby liked because it sounded like the title of a book of essays by F. R. Leavis and suggested a picture of teachers casting off their shackles and striding off towards a bright horizon, beyond which lay happiness, freedom, fulfilment . . .

The rest will be familiar to readers of the educational press ('In-house investigation: the way forward for secondary?'); the posh broadsheets ('He doesn't look like an electrician. And he isn't!'); the rabid tabloids ('Sir grasses up his mates'); viewers of daytime TV ('And coming up after the break, the amazing story of how two teachers escaped the chalkface to . . .').

The speed of their success amazed them. Almond stayed at Dog Lane till the end of the year, then resigned. He was able to do this because – on the basis of three small ads in the *Times Ed*, a modest website and a whirlwind of word-of-mouth recommendations – they found they were both working flat out all day and every day (and charging what they liked).

The thing had its own momentum. People they investigated clamoured to join the firm. People who took them on begged to join as well. Their growth was sensational. After a year they had a full-time team of a hundred dedicated professional ex-teachers travelling the length and breadth of the country pretending to be insignificant supply teachers. When the word got around they had to vary their approach. Teachers, they found, are also brilliant actors. They became electricians, cutting plastic sheaths from wiring while leaning over to catch the gossip about someone, or plumbers poking in the sink as teachers milled around making coffee.

Money poured in. Almond moved to a huge place in that mysterious part of Birmingham just north of the university. It had ten bedrooms (or eleven, he was never sure exactly), and a garden which was more like a small country park. He offered the gatehouse to Lazenby, but he declined the offer, saying he was happier with something a bit smaller;

he bought a four-bedroomed place in a leafy Harborne cul-de-sac instead. Also instead, Almond let his morose in-laws stay in the gatehouse whenever their curiosity overcame their envy and they came to visit.

After two years they had a permanent staff of five hundred or so, and an ever-growing army of part-timers. It was all getting a bit out of control. If it had been allowed to continue, Lazenby thought, they would have had to start franchising. Gradually it began to dawn on him that there was a logical conclusion beyond which their enterprise could not go.

And he wasn't the only one.

One glorious summer day Lazenby was relaxing at home when the phone rang. It was Almond.

'Tim. There's a man here.'

'What kind of man?'

'Just come. Please.'

'What does this man want?'

'Us. He wants us. A man. Sitting here, looking at me.'

Lazenby could sense a creeping loss of control. It was something he'd sensed in Almond before. 'Just calm down. Now, tell me slowly, is he from somewhere – you know, official?'

Lazenby heard a whimper at the other end of the phone. It told him everything. He'd always known this day would come. 'I'll be right there,' he said.

Lazenby took the BMW, leaving the Porsche at home. It was silly to be ostentatious at a time like this. Five minutes later he was parking it next to the row of Almond's four-by-fours, crunching over his drive, marching through his foyer, striding across the expanse of his drawing room towards the figure who rose from the armchair, a long arm outstretched before him. He was tall, spindly and dressed like a bank manager in a 1950s film. There was something very familiar in the set of his teeth as he smiled in greeting. Lazenby couldn't pin it down at first. Then it came to him: Alec Guinness in *The Ladykillers*.

'Mr Lazenby. At last,' he said, smiling towards each of them in turn. 'Well, it's so good to have caught you both.'

There was a period of great silence. Stillness. And staring. Great staring.

'Oh, I'm so sorry. Did I say "caught you"? I meant, caught *up* with you. Hn hn hn hn hn,' he chuckled through his teeth.

Almond was speechless. Lazenby, on the other hand, found himself prattling away like a Jane Austen character.

'You appear to have the advantage of us, sir –'

'I'm so sorry. I did mention my name to Mr Almond here, but he appears to have forgotten.'

They both stared at Almond.

'Yes,' he went on. 'Anyway, let me introduce myself . . . again. My name is Edward Arbogast and I work for the government.'

The effect of this on Almond was fairly dramatic. He might just as well have said he worked for the Gestapo.

'Which bit?' said Lazenby.

'All of me.'

'No, I meant which bit of the government?'

'Well, how long have you got?' said Arbogast.

'A very long time,' said Lazenby, wearily.

'Okay. Well, I'm a bit of a jack-of-all-trades really. I report to a number of permanent secretaries, under-secretaries, heads of sections; I can hardly keep track of it all myself sometimes. There's Employment, Inland Revenue, VAT, Customs and Excise, Benefits and, of course, Education.'

Every one of these words hit them like bullets. But particularly, for some reason, *sections*. Spies always worked in a *section*, didn't they? Lazenby thought they'd better get to the end of this before Almond fainted. Or worse.

Arbogast saw their speechlessness and pressed on.

'I'll come straight to the point. You two have been very busy for the last few years and have obviously,' he said, looking round as the maid (or it might have been the nanny) popped in, stared at them, then disappeared, 'reaped the benefits. But I'm afraid, gentlemen, that all good things must come to an end.'

'Again, sir, you have the advantage of us.'

'Yes, well, as I said, to the point. This – thing – you've set up is in breach of a list of regulations as long as . . .' he groped for an appropriate comparison as he gazed out of the french windows, 'as your back garden, Mr Almond. VAT, Income Tax, National Insurance, Corporation Tax, Employment Laws, Pensions, Health and Safety, benefit fraud, avoidances, evasions . . .' At this point he took a notebook from his inside pocket and peered into it. 'For instance, a hundred and eight-two of the eight hundred and seventy-nine people you currently employ full-time –'

'How many?' shouted Lazenby, as much because he wanted to cover up Almond's groan of despair as out of a desire to know.

'Eight hundred and seventy-nine,' replied Arbogast calmly. 'Why? Did you think there were more?'

'I didn't think it was so many.'

'Funny how things creep up on you, isn't it? That's why you really should keep proper records. Anyway, a hundred and eight-two of them are also claiming substantial benefits. And they are able to do so undetected because you don't obey one single employment law regulation.'

There was another great silence. And another great staring.

'I'll tell you what I'll do,' he said.

Almond spoke at last. He turned his face to Lazenby in a caricature of slavering gratitude. 'The man,' he said. 'He'll tell us what he'll do.'

'Yes I will,' said Arbogast patiently. 'I'm not going to do anything about the several hundred laws you've violated, and for which you could go to prison for many years, *and* pay several thousand pounds in back-payments and fines. No. I'm not going to do a thing about any of that. What I particularly want to straighten out is the effect you are having on the education system of this country.'

'I hardly think so,' said Lazenby.

'Well, just think a bit more,' said Arbogast.

Lazenby again gave it as his opinion that, notwithstanding the recent expansion of their activities, no lasting detrimental effect could, as yet, be detected on the aforementioned education system.

'You may not think so,' replied Arbogast eventually, 'but I deal in real figures, not idle suppositions. The logical conclusion of what you are doing will be a disaster. Schools will be staffed entirely by youngsters who can't control kids, old fogeys who don't give a toss and cynical subversives who work for you. Sorry to be so blunt.'

'No problem.'

'You see, for all its faults, the system does what it's supposed to do. It regulates the flow and direction of people into the empty spaces that continually need filling up. Every year we need so many doctors, so many plumbers, so many filing clerks, Professors of Medieval Italian, civil servants, policemen . . . need I go on? And if proper teachers are running off in droves, leaving only a collection of childminders to handle an increasingly difficult school population of disaffected psychopaths . . . you can see our problem.'

'But don't you think you're partly responsible? I mean, teachers wouldn't be queuing up to join us if they were allowed to teach instead of filling in forms all day long and going to endless pointless meetings, and writing pointless reports and enduring pointless inspections.'

Arbogast lifted his hands. 'Absolutely. I couldn't agree with you more. If it was up to me, schools would just serve up a bit of Latin, a bit of Greek, a bit of Maths, some English, some Science, spotted dick for tea, evening prep, endless games of cricket . . .' He gazed out at the sunny expanse of Almond's lawn. 'Yes, well, it's not up to me. I have to do as I'm told, I'm afraid. Orders is orders. I am authorized to put a proposal to you.'

'We'll do anything,' whispered Almond.

'We don't want a fuss. You two have achieved quite a high profile over the past couple of years. We just want you to let everything stop, and not say anything, not to the papers, the media, anybody. Not ever. And in return, we leave you alone.'

'We'll do anything.'

'You mean,' said Lazenby, laying a hand on Almond's arm, 'we just switch off the website and disappear?'

'Actually,' said Arbogast, looking at his watch, 'the website was switched off four minutes ago. As I said, we don't want a fuss. You say nothing, and you can keep all this and there'll be no . . . unpleasantness.'

'We'll do anything.'

III

Two years passed. It was Christmas Day. Lazenby was sitting at home, still in Harborne. He had prepared and eaten a traditional lunch. This was it, he thought: his own nest, worn to his own shape, where he could lie, purring and contented, for the rest of his days.

He was sipping a rather energetic, single-minded Merlignac and sucking a pensive, but adventurous Niejmurer panatella and contemplating the prospect of the energetic,

single-minded, pensive and adventurous sex he would probably have later with the owner of the voice which was carelessly singing, nay, *trilling*, in the kitchen as she prepared
coffee.

Jane ran her own fashion business. Lazenby thought he
might marry Jane one day. Jane thought she might marry
Lazenby. But there was no hurry. Since the end of New
Departures he had met many people like Jane: people who
worked for themselves, people who did what they wanted.
New Departures had given him an introduction into the
world of freelance journalism, television, after-dinner speaking and, most profitably, the motivational workshop racket.
It was truly amazing how much money people were willing
to part with, just for the privilege of listening to him spouting what was nothing more than vapid drivel.

He was watching telly. *The Great Escape*. The familiar
images unrolled: Steve McQueen trying to fly over the barbed
wire on his motorbike; Charles Bronson going tunnel-crazy;
that little Scottish bloke (who was later in *Crossroads*)
going stir-crazy, and later wire-crazy; that bloke out of *The
Professionals*, and before that *Upstairs, Downstairs*, forgetting to speak German and running like a madman through
that nice little German town with Richard Attenborough.

And as he watched, he noticed something for the first
time. Throughout the film, the weather is lovely. The whole
thing is bathed in sharp Alpine sunlight and the nights are
clear and starry. It's always July and August.

And the camp is lovely too. They've got all these clubs
and societies. Gardening, bird-watching, singing, printing,
clothes-making and, of course, tunnelling. This isn't prison
camp by Dostoevsky, but by Richmal Crompton. It's like
the third form at a public school in Dorset. Everybody is a
good chap. Even the Germans are chaps, in different uniforms. Even the *tunnels* are chaps!

Lazenby began to understand something very profound, something involving the essential contradiction in being human. He began to see the film, and life, in a new light.

They don't want to escape. The camp *is* the escape. What are the alternatives? Tramp round occupied Europe, cold and terrified, hiding in ditches? Return to their loved ones, and find out they've been sleeping with the butcher for a few extra chops? Get back to flying flimsy planes over cities and blasting people to bits? Crikey! Give over! Not likely! No fear!

They have to try, of course. It's expected. But only in a pantomime kind of way. 'For you the war is over,' the Germans insist. 'Oh no it isn't!' reply our chaps. But it is.

Their loved ones are with them in the camp, digging their tunnels, forging their documents, making uniforms out of rags, creating diversions, bribing guards. They've already escaped. The light is fulgent. They have PT all day and study at night. Occasionally they're allowed to ride a motorbike and maybe finish a tunnel.

Lazenby understood. He understood why people buy lottery tickets, why they write letters to papers then wait gleefully all week to see if they've been printed, why they get married and have children. They are trying to escape, to burst through into another, more glowing world; but they don't really want to in the end, because that would leave them nothing to hope for.

Where did all the people in New Departures go? What did they want?

Suddenly he saw the light. It was the same light, he was sure, that filled the minds of people like Newton, Plato and Shakespeare, when they first received an inkling of the broad idea which would direct their every thought for the rest of their lives: not a stark light, allowing tiny details to be seen, but a soft, encompassing luminescence, highlighting only some parts of the broad mental landscape which spread before him.

And an image swam, complete and unbidden, into his vision. He was in some sort of wooden hut. There was a crude stove. He lifted it to reveal a hole in the floor. There was so much to do – dispose of the soil, get light and ventilation down there and possibly a little railway, forge official stamps – well, we could use bits of old shoe leather and black polish. So much work. So much ingenuity.

As Jane came in with the coffee, Lazenby said, 'I've just got to make a quick phone call.'

Joan Michelson

JOAN MICHELSON grew up in America and settled in England. She teaches Creative Writing at Birkbeck College, University of London. Her poems, essays and fiction have been published in magazines and anthologies, including *New Writing 14* (Granta, 2006). Her poetry chapbook, *Letting in the Light*, was Editor's Choice publication with Poeticmatrix Press (USA, 2002). She won first prize in Londonarts International Poetry Competition, 2005.

To Catch a Thief

Joan Michelson

In the 1990s before Starbucks, Costa Coffee and other specialist cafés opened on the Broadway, for morning coffee we stopped at 7-Eleven. We could have done worse. Open twenty-four hours a day, seven days a week, the corner shop could be relied upon for light and warmth, and it was well stocked with essentials: newspapers, cigarettes, toothpaste, condoms and ready-meals.

7-Eleven had bought out that long-enduring icon, Lyons Corner House, and there were new security glass windows on adjoining sides. One faced a Victorian pub, a fine stout building with panels of smoked glass set in an oak door; the other and most important for this story, the new face of Lloyds Bank, glass with marble-clad stone enclosing two self-service cash machines. With the new machines, available twenty-four hours a day, had come new forms and new heights of card theft.

Government-pushed, our local police set out to crack all crime, and especially card theft. Their plan was 'community action': to rouse us to save the area from turning into a no-go zone and sending property prices down the sewers. It was a forward-looking idea. In our own way, we took to it. We formed a 7-Eleven Watch Committee and dedicated ourselves to watching the shop manager, Mr Sung. If there was a model for us to study, he was it: thief-chaser, thief-catcher and a thief. Following him, we watched the bank and kept a better eye on who was behind us.

The first time I saw Mr Sung, he was involved in a chase. A man the size of an elf, he was running uphill after three six-foot-something teenagers, two black, one white. The hoodlums were on their lunch break from St Martin's secondary school over the hill and they had helped themselves to supplies from 7-Eleven. Ten minutes later, I had a chance to observe the man close up. His hair plastered to his skull, his face blotchy, his chest heaving and shirt sticking to him, he went about his business. He returned the goods to their assigned places: the sliced white to the bread shelf, the large bag of onion crisps to the snacks, the tins of Coke to the drinks refrigerator. Then he wiped at himself with a handkerchief and went behind the counter for a pack of Mayfair.

There wasn't very much to him: bones strung together under a thin layer of skin with veins standing out. He had scars the length of his arm like a map to a secret and in the elbow folds a web-work of dots and lines.

'Aren't you afraid?' I asked him. 'What if one of those guys pulled a knife on you?'

'Nobody trick Mr Sung,' he said. He added with more care, his voice lowered, the words spread out, 'If they have a knife, they better use it. If I see that knife, I'm going to grab it and I'm going to cut off their hands.'

Before long, I'd found out that he was a 'boat person' from Vietnam. The story was that he had been lucky. After three days squeezed into a fishing boat built for three and carrying thirty-three, just sitting, no food, no water, and all the time cloudy in the head, he had been picked up by a British freighter. It was enormous. It even had a swimming pool. In five days, he was on the other side of the South

China Sea; in three more months, flown out of Singapore. The UK was okay. No wars. You could learn English. You could have an education. The policemen were nice and had no guns. From the refugee centre, he had been resettled in an abandoned army camp in North Staffordshire. He did not mind the army camp, but he didn't want to live in the countryside. It was too much quiet, he told us. He was hearing the cuckoo saying 'cuckoo, cuckoo'. But it was there that he met his wife and that his twins were born.

Our singer, Ariadne, who sorts clothes for the Oxfam shop, was convinced Mr Sung had come down to London for work: so he could send money home to his wife. Our greengrocer, Georgiou, agreed with Ariadne. But Peter, our philosopher, who runs at least five miles a day with his baby in a backpack, thought Mr Sung had something else going on in London. But then Peter liked things to be complicated; he liked to think about complicated life situations. Not Sean. Sean was a gentleman of the road. He argued that if you didn't have the facts, and we didn't, you should keep your nose clean. I, resettled American, could see his point. All that we knew for certain was that Mr Sung worked all hours and, as the new girl from Hong Kong, the one in the blue specs, said, 'Is wound up too tight.'

Personally I didn't think Mr Sung had time for anything else in London or anywhere. He told me that he hadn't had a day off since he started. He couldn't go home. He couldn't even go to the toilet because staff didn't show up. He couldn't go out for a cigarette because the moment he did, cigarettes walked out. One day, in a bag, two thousand. He reported the number to the police and they made a note for their file.

'Where is time?' Mr Sung asked me, more than once. 'In a job like this – twenty-four hours a day seven days a week.

I have it up to my neck.' He pressed the side of his hand to his neck like a blade for a swift cut.

'Maybe you should pack it in,' I said, talking lightly like someone in a cowboy film. 'Go rob a bank.'

Our 7-Eleven Watch went on for as long as Mr Sung was our hero. We had this to say for him: by the time he left, we knew how to pick up the chase, retrieve and put right. Here's one success out of the seven we marked up during those months. Georgiou's father, Demetrious, had finally let go and the old high-built bed had to go too because the house was going to be sold. Georgiou gathered up the shoes that had been under the bed for a lifetime: a dozen of his father's and more than a dozen of his mother's. Dozens. He paired them, tied or buckled partners to one another, and packed them in black bin bags which he closed and knotted tightly. By the time he found all of them, under the couch and under the armchair too, he had five black bin bags. They filled the back of his Ford Escort. Because it was already night, he left them in the car to take to the charity shop the next morning. Locking up, he thought, amused: No one would have a clue what was in the bags. A couple of hours later some local hoodlums came sauntering by. They noticed the car with stuff in it. One of them found a broken brick, another a weight of concrete. So they smashed the windows to get the stuff out.

Georgiou is a deep and regular sleeper, out like a light by ten so he can be up at four to get to New Covent Garden and back in time to unload and set up his shop. At one in the morning, he was sound asleep but Peter, jogging with the baby, was making one of his night rounds. He passed Georgiou's car just in time to give chase. He closed in on the hoodlums and took possession of the bags. The baby on his back, a man-size bag to his chest, he made five trips to the Oxfam shop on the Broadway. His route took him past 7-Eleven where Mr Sung sat, a lone counterman on watch, and past Georgiou's Fruit & Vegetables with the metal door pulled tight to the paving and padlocked to an iron hook. The bags were standing there untouched when Ariadne arrived to open up the charity shop at nine-thirty the next morning.

The theft and recapture of the Papadopoulos shoes was the talk of the day. Mr Sung was unusually congratulatory. With a wink at Peter, as if including him in a secret, Mr Sung said, 'Nobody trick Mr Sung Watch.' Smiling and nodding, he looked around, checking on his shop in his customary way. We left him there while we nipped over to the pub. We hadn't meant any harm going without him, but I guess we did enough because he was waiting with a litany of complaints. He could never do anything he wanted. The boss kept saying he'd have a break. The boss kept promising to arrange cover. 'This is the break I get,' Mr Sung snarled. 'No break.' But there was worse. As soon as we had crossed to the pub, the boss had rung and accused him of a mistake in the invoice.

We didn't think of it as anything much but, in fact, it was the end. As he told us, his face changed and his voice shifted up a register. The words practically sang themselves. 'Today I am writing my letter of resignation.'

Mr Sung disappeared so fast it was as if we were the butt of a confidence trick. In a way we were. But first we were kept in ignorance. The next week there was a new counter girl, a heavy young woman from Hong Kong who wore new-fashion big round spectacles in blue frames. She didn't know anything about our hero. Nor did the replacement manager, a lad from the Midlands who had come straight from the Dublin campus of McDonald's College of Management.

Then one day, we caught his boss, manager of UK South-east. He was a clean-cut, pale-faced thirty-year-old who looked like the McDonald's graduate's older brother. First he tried to brush us off with the story of his own hardships. He himself had more than enough to deal with to keep track of the likes of a Mr Sung. Fifty-three shops. He lived on the road. When did he get to see his wife? His kid?

We didn't give up. We wanted to know. All right, he allowed, he supposed Mr Sung had some problems. Some outside problems. As we held our ground, we could see the colour rising in his face. He wanted us gone and he didn't want to lose it. He lowered his voice in stages until we were forced to lip-read words he had been forbidden to say aloud. 'Sung said he put the money through the slot. Three thousand quid. Vanished without trace.'

Last summer I thought I saw the elfin thief darting out of Leicester Square station and into the wilds of Chinatown. As I started after him, the words I had thrown out so casually repeated in my mind like a cuckoo call. 'Go rob a bank. Go rob a bank.' I felt as if I had ordered him to do it. I was the criminal behind the criminal. For a moment the spur of my conscience caught me in the throat. What had I done? Then I was overtaken by rage. What had he done? I was on him like a mad thing, only it was not Mr Sung. But this man flashed a blade sharp enough to cut off my hands.

An Ace in the Midlands
Joan Michelson

I

November 23, 1974

Dear People,
   It's your Joey, back in England where he started four months ago, back from Barcelona, Paris, Copenhagen, Helsinki, Turku and a voyage by Russian boat across the Baltic Sea and the North Sea and up the mouth of the Thames. Everyone on the boat was Russian or Polish and took him for Polish and no one spoke English.

So let me remind you of the Joys of English. English-English or American-English, it is Home Sweet Home to me.

And hey-hi there from this Home Sweet Home where you Mind Your Step. Right now, eight p.m. on a foggy November night, I am minding my step deep in the heart of the nation in a place called Hobbles End. I am sitting in a classroom in St Mary's Infant–Junior School, the Hobbles End Infant–Junior School, teaching a class; or I would be teaching if there were anyone here to teach. I came up from London this afternoon. It's not a bad journey: two hours and a bit, Euston to Birmingham, and the stopping train through Duddeston, Snaresville and Castleville and three or four other towns to this one which doesn't end so much as drop into a valley of defunct mines. With a Mining Museum somewhere around.

Mining for another time. Today it's Adult Education. How does this story go? Is there a hero? Does he make any money? About the money, never mind. This is a visitor's experience of the Old World from yours truly, Joseph W. Schechter-Greene.

It starts like this. Looking for work along professional lines, I make my way into the West End to the City Literary Institute which is in an old building that in its day might have been something. I climb six flights of stairs to a one-person office. It is dark with varnished wood and dark because the lighting is kept at a conservative wattage, an Old World characteristic I've come to recognize. In the dim light I face a superior being. Her name is Eleanor Rose, MPhil. She is tall with glittering earrings and a matching pin holding a silk scarf against her throat. She's wearing a silky white blouse with blousy sleeves and, in a ray cast from her angled desk lamp, the buttons that run between her breasts gleam like gems. This is as much as I get to see because she's seated behind a solid Victorian desk and I am seated in front of it. Nothing else is very clear. She could be thirty. She could be fifty. She could be a lot of things I can't guess at.

She asks me for the information I gave her on the phone and in the letter I submitted as she directed. For the third time I explain that I have a Master of Fine Arts degree in creative writing from an American university, and that I'm interested in running a writing class. She repeats that she is interested and that she would like to take the matter a bit further. She asks me if I'm willing to travel. I tell her, 'I'll go anywhere as long as British Rail can get me there.'

At this she smiles as if I've said an endearing thing.

'It's a great trip. A chance to see the real England,' I add.

She nods and smiles again, as if she agrees that neither she nor London is quite the real thing. She says that British Rail goes just about everywhere, doesn't it? Then she quotes somebody at me, Robert Louis Stevenson in fact. 'To travel hopefully is a better thing than to arrive.' Without explaining what she means or intends, she draws the interview to a close. She stands up, revealing a long dark skirt that fits perfectly, not too close, not too loose, over her impressive hips. She says that she has greatly enjoyed meeting me and that she'll come back to me in a couple of days.

I think that's the end of it but the next morning at nine, I'm called to the communal phone which beeps at intervals as if in want of money. It's Eleanor Rose. A slot has opened up for a class starting at six that evening. Am I interested? Sure I'm interested.

A few minutes later her colleague, Harry Noble, rings from Birmingham. The thing is, they've lost a tutor at short notice. Harry Noble doesn't tell me what happened to the tutor. When we meet, I notice that he's lost a finger and I wonder how it happened. But he doesn't invite questions, personal or other. He has a lot to say and he says it, keeping to the topics of money and forms. They have to make a special case to the Home Office for employing an American. The argument is that I won't be doing a job the Brits could do themselves. While we're waiting to hear, they won't be able to process my fee claims. This means they won't be able to pay me.

'Whatever you say,' I tell him. 'Okay.'

'It will get you a foot in the door,' he says.

'My foot in the door is worth two in the mouth,' I say, making a joke. He treats it as if I haven't opened my mouth or as if he's heard the saying too many times or as if he hasn't heard it at all. Maybe he hasn't because he's bent over a map he's decorating with red arrows so I can find my way from Hobbles End rail station to the school. When I get there I should find a large envelope with the name Robin Todds waiting in the tray on the table. I have to take the attendance each week and initial my student numbers or I can't be paid – whenever I do get paid, if I do get paid, which depends on the Home Office.

I found the school, one of those tall cavernous brick buildings set behind a forbidding iron fence. I found the register, a cardboard folder with empty blue lines with squares along the bottom for my initials. And I found room 3a with lidded wooden desks, the old-fashioned kind with a groove for a pen and a hole for an inkpot. I squeezed in and sat for a few moments, trying to re-enter my childhood. Mine took place pretty far away but the students, if they could squeeze in, would be back at their own old desks. If they couldn't, we might sit on top of the desks, I thought. But the first student to arrive came in staggering under a stack of metal chairs.

As soon we'd arranged the chairs, as if waiting for us to get the job done, the other seven came through the door. Personal flair showed in hand-knit scarves. Otherwise they wore uniform tops and bottoms, light with dark, blouses and shirts, skirts and trousers. There was one exception, a young woman named Serena. She was into Indian cotton and velvets and had one of those long-skirted ethnic dresses with little mirrors that glint like mica.

As soon as I'd introduced myself, they wanted to know what part of the States I was from or was it a Canadian accent they detected. How did I spell my name? And could they have a list of the books I've written?

I could have entertained them with my story of Hope for Tomorrow or Law No. 2 that Death Comes Before

Publishing, but I wanted to get the session under way. 'This isn't about my writing,' I said. 'This is about yours.'

I wrote the names in the register. Mr C. Duckworth-Babb, Mrs L. Briggs, Mrs S. Bronx-Henchy, Mrs J. Proudlove, Mr T. Lawless, Mrs G. Radford, Mrs E. Tittensor and Mrs P. Wilton. I wrote the date, marked an X for each student present, signed my initials in the box at the bottom and felt that I was on my way. I looked up. 'Who's brought what to read?' I looked around the circle. They were looking at their hands. No one had brought anything or no one was going to admit to anything.

'Well, okay,' I said and gave a little clap. 'What would you like to write?' No one said anything. I could feel the silence gel, then freeze. I could feel my mind on the verge of an ice age. 'Okay.' I changed direction. 'I guess being the first night maybe we should jibber-jabber.' They looked at me as if I was speaking a foreign language. 'Jibber-jabber. Gossip. Chit-chat. Talk.'

Suddenly it was easy. They knew how to talk. I asked questions and they answered all at once. In another minute, I was surreptitiously getting details down for the Little Book To Be.

Three of the women write the church newsletter. Jenny, Eleanor and Serena. One of the guys is an accountant. That's Charles Duckworth-Babb. There's a young married, Lily Briggs, who makes tents in her garage. Her husband directs the church choir. Lily said, quote, Thursday is her Night Out and Roger jolly well better have the little devils asleep before she gets home. She has four under the age of six and is four months on with numbers five and six. Gwynne Radford has three rising teens and she makes dolls with porcelain limbs and heads and rag bodies and also rag dolls, rag rugs and teddies. From her home business she makes the money for the housekeeping, for family holidays abroad and for her evening classes. Number eight is the older man, the one who came staggering in with the stack of chairs and helped arrange them in a circle. He's used to it. He used to teach botany at the local College of Agriculture. Also, he saw the war in the Far East and had the privilege of being a prisoner under the Japanese.

Lawless isn't the only one who remembers the Second World War. Tittensor was a schoolgirl and so was Radford. Those were the days. Out for a bike ride after school and black Americans were all over the place throwing them Hershey chocolate bars. Then there's the German bomb that hit the castle. Well, it was already a ruin. But then there was the shell-shock. Lawless had a lot to say about shell-shock and about a few other things like marriage and divorce, his sweet peas about which he could have elaborated for hours. And he had to tell us his father's favourite about coming home from the previous war, tripping over a paving stone in front of his own house and breaking an arm and a leg.

From war stories, we progressed to holiday catastrophes. Lily Briggs, the pregnant tentmaker, took the floor. Her face was on fire and she giggled before and after and in the middle of her two gems. First was family camping on the Welsh coast. They watched one of her own tents, six days' work, sail off a cliff side and everything that was in it sail after it. The odd thing was, it sounded like a bomb exploding. 'You'd think it was the starting gun for the next world war.' She laughed her giggle. Next, Uncle Justin and Aunt Hilda had a burst pipe. They had merrily gone off on holiday to Mallorca to one of those hotels with fancy swimming pools and come home to their own Hobbles End pool. They hadn't been in the house five minutes before Uncle Justin opened the door to the basement and practically drowned. It had risen all the way to the ground floor. No one asked what happened next but she told us. She said, 'Aunt Hilda had to call the police.' She stumbled. 'Police-plumber.'

'The plumber-police,' I cut in. 'Well done. Great. That's the stuff. You got it. It sounds like nothing but it's something. Take Uncle Justin,' I expanded, waxing a little lyrical. 'From the chlorine blue waters of hotel Spain to the tea-brown of Hobbles End. The plumbing-police get a chance to go fishing. Think about it.' Did they understand? I wasn't sure. They seemed to be staring at me. 'I mean, you have stories. Go home and write. Write it before you lose it. Hurry up and get it down. And come back. I can't wait to read what you've written.' They were still sitting there. 'Well, you can stay here and do it,' I said, collecting my things and going to the door. 'Get started. See you next week.'

That was the first week. Now it's the sixth. I'm writing because I'm here on my own; and I'm writing this because I am here. Technically I'm not here any longer. I have been dismissed, but I need to sit here to write these things down before I forget. I'm afraid I've been blessed with one of those come-and-go memories. I leave a place, I forget what happened. I come back, I remember.

Week two: I was cockeyed with great expectations, ready to promote their work, warming up my reviews and inventing little mottos to share with them. From now on we'd be in it together, trying the writer's life. 'Shoulder to the wheel,' I practised under my breath, 'but pen to the stars.'

This time five out of the eight showed up. I looked around. 'Five stories. Who wants to get it over with? Free the fear. Then you can really listen to the others. Believe me, I know. I've been there. Fear-full. First is best and worst. Okay?' I looked around.

Did they have excuses and were they long-winded. It was such a busy week. So many unexpected things. So many interruptions. Mrs Tittensor's Nigel flushed his spectacles down the loo which meant he was home from school until they could get him another pair. They had to go to the GP for a referral to the eye clinic and what with the forms and the queues and the kinds of things she had to do to keep Nigel out of mischief, that was the week gone. Then, on the weekend, she had to lead a search party. A not so very old neighbour was losing her marbles. This time she'd really lost them and was all the way in the soup. The stink-house soup. Animal waste works. Mrs Tittensor went on to give us a rundown on the recycling plant, which is a big local issue. No one wants it anywhere near the town. Trucks go trundling through in the middle of the night and leave a stench that lasts for days.

There was a debate about how many days, then a discussion about wind direction. After that Lawless gave a report on the breakdown of his daughter's marriage. He wasn't altogether sparing of details. He was hanging wallpaper when she phoned from Bradford. Her mother had shopped around in Birmingham and brought home some rolls of the new fabric-look. It had a sheen. Gave a bit of shine in the dark which would save on the night lights possibly. They'd have to test it out. But it was a bit pricey. So his daughter phoned from the bungalow they'd recently purchased outside of Bradford, a good fifteen miles out, and begged him to come right away; she had to come home. It took him half the day to get her, and the stuff she'd packed up meant he was going to have to make at least one more trip up there. Between the packing boxes and keeping the roof rack from slipping was another story and a half. Well, that was his writing time gone.

In the Wilton home, it was flu week. As for Gwynne Radford, her kitten had gone missing and she had Mother staying.

I did what I could. I changed the name of the class to Creative Reading. 'What are you reading for pleasure? Which books are *your* books?'

They seemed more comfortable with this. 'The Bible,' they began. 'Shakespeare. Daffodils.'

'Anything more modern?' These came fast.

'Rudyard Kipling. Somerset Maugham, Thomas Hardy, Graham Greene.'

'From our time?'

'Fay Weldon,' someone said.

'Ah,' I said, to cover my ignorance. 'And she wrote?'

'I'm thinking of *Down Among the Women*.' This came from the one who wore the skirt with mirrors in it, a bit of a bohemian maybe, maybe from somewhere else, another world, some other England. She spoke in a different way, more London but not London. She articulated beautifully, dauntingly. Mrs Bronx-Henchy. Serena. A young woman who dressed differently. She continued in a sweet low voice. The words tripped out at speed.

'That was one book that had a liberating effect on me. There's another book I read recently,' she said and then, hardly pausing, 'Are you from New York?'

'Sort of.'

'Maybe you know the author. Erica Jong.'

This took me by surprise. In fact, I did know the author. Or I had seen the author. Or I had heard the author because the auditorium in the city (New York City) was jam-packed with liberated women. Short though I am (in my school days pushed to the front of the group for line-ups), for this reading, I was exiled to the back. It was some performance. She is some writer. It's some book. Chaucer revisited by blonde American Jewish Ph.D. student married to an American psychotherapist from Chinatown. He was right there in the back with the rest of us, listening to her therapeutic fiction. Husband and lover romp through Europe and end up in the same bed on the same night. She let it all hang out and covered herself. The shared night in the shared bed was forgotten like a dream that never happened and that no one mentioned. As if it hadn't happened. But it had happened. Sex and more sex. Or in her happy turn of phrase, fantastic for book sales, 'the zipless fuck'.

Was this a text to assign my students in Hobbles End? *Fear of Flying* with its zipless fuck for church newsletter ladies? More than half the students were born before the war. Beyond that, the way I saw it, the journey to Hobbles End was a journey back in time about half a century. I looked at Serena. Did she know what she was saying? Was there something in her I was failing to see? Was she an agent for the other? For another? She smiled what appeared to be a genuine warm smile. She looked both inviting and serene. On the other hand, we were in a building that was the property of the Church of England. For all I knew, the walls had ears.

I thought this might be one way to lose my job. On the other hand, how much of a job was it to lose? Was she baiting me? Was I too fearful to rise? I decided I was game. 'Okay. We'll do it. *Fear of Flying* for next week,' I said. 'Read it and we'll talk.'

'The whole book?'

'Try it for bedtime reading,' I said, then thought I shouldn't have. I remembered the Dumas quote about the bonds of wedlock being heavy weights and sometimes needing three to carry them. To cover myself I turned to Serena and asked her to lead the discussion.

'I'm counting on you,' I threw at her and assumed it was agreed.

Perhaps it was, but I shouldn't have counted on Serena. I shouldn't have counted on any of them. Or rather any of them except old man Lawless, who applies his British army training to his daily life. He'd driven up to Bradford again. He'd found three copies of the book in the carousel in the rail station. He would have bought them for the others if anyone had mentioned it or had he thought of it. That meant that when the class started we had two copies of the book, because I'd found one in my local library, which was next door to Keats's House.

Creative Reading. Week three.

I'd read my Erica Jong and made enough notes for a *TLS* essay and a book chapter, or maybe a whole book of chapters. Connections fly through my head. I wonder what Serena saw. I arrived early, hoping she would be there so we could talk about it. I wondered what was in the book that made her think of it, how she saw herself in relation to the heroine, Isadora Wing, how she fit into Women's Liberation. But Serena didn't show up early.

No one showed up early, but Mr Lawless was there on the dot and helped me set up the chairs. We sat down opposite one another in the circle at the back and he noticed a hole in the window behind me. It looked like someone had shot at it with a BB gun.

'Walls with ears, windows with eyes, what is this world coming to?' I asked in a teasing tone.

Mr Lawless took it straight. 'It's the new generation. They have no respect for anything.' He went on the way older people do about when he was growing up and how people behaved before the war until he'd heard enough of his own voice. Then he took his book out and, saying that he had a few more pages to read, which seemed a shrinking of the truth, unless he was taking it in reverse order, he started reading. I walked over to the window and looked through the BB gun hole at the dark grass in the empty play area. Where was Serena?

When Eleanor Tittensor arrived, she explained that Serena couldn't make it and she sent her apologies. 'What happened?' Eleanor avoided answering and she and the other two ladies, Jenny Proudlove and Gywnne Radford, dissembled for a while. They told us they hadn't read the book because they hadn't been able to get it. Gwynne had made it into Birmingham on Monday and she'd intended to stop in the bookshop but there was a signal failure so the train got her in fifty minutes late and what with one thing or another, it turned out to be a nightmare and when she stepped off the train in Hobbles End, she realized she'd forgotten the book.

Then, as if they'd suddenly been liberated and ordered to assert themselves, they let me have it, the story of the Book Burning.

'I gave it good go.' Eleanor defended herself. 'I made myself sit in my chair and read right through to the end of chapter one. Frankly, to tell the truth, that Chinese lady has some nerve. In my opinion, this is disgusting filthy rubbish. Without wanting to cause offence,' she said, 'I don't think this is a book that any decent family would want on their shelves. I had a good mind to chuck it into the dustbin but what about those lust-abouts rummaging through the rubbish, my conscience told me, *Eleanor Tittensor, you throw it on the fire.*'

Mr Babb had missed the previous session and didn't know the import or impact. 'Duck,' he said, which he called all the women, Duck or Duckie, depending on degrees of intimacy or distancing. He was disapproving, so it was Duck. 'The next time you're low on fuel, call on me and I'll bring a bag over.' He turned to me and apologized. 'As a rule, Mr Schechter, the British don't burn books.'

I did what I could to get through the second hour. What I could do was talk. I talked about Alexander Pope and decorum and send-ups and satire. I talked about dreams, about Sigmund Freud who died not very far from where I'm renting my basement room. I talked about *Don Quixote* and *Candide* and myth and Lord Byron. I went on to Women's Liberation, the big Coming Out in New York, the Women-for-Women Revolution, Women-Against-Men. Men were diminished, dismissed, ignored and learned to compromise. I talked about how hard it is to be a man in New York given what's happened to the women. I encouraged all of them to think about visiting New York, to think about staying there for a while. New York was a world unto itself, I told them. You have to keep pushing at the boundaries of your life and of your way of thinking. I told them, 'You too can rebirth yourself in a bathtub.'

Then I got a little carried away. 'I want you to think about this. Ask yourself "Do these words deserve to be burnt?"' I started reading out loud from the book and, crazy as this sounds, I felt that Erica's words could be my own. 'Whatever happened I knew I would survive it. I knew, above all, that I'd go on working. Surviving meant being born over and over. It wasn't easy and it was always painful. But there wasn't any other choice except death.'

Week number four. Only two showed up, not Eleanor Tittensor nor Mr Babb nor the spot-on-time Mr Lawless. It was the ladies, Jenny Proudlove and Serena Bronx-Henchy. They were physically present so I marked them present but they had not come for Creative Writing or Creative Reading. After a brief hello, they left me alone in the circle and settled down on the other side of the room to deal with their business. They were quite a pair: Proudlove straight and trim in sensible skirt and blouse with her hair cut in bowl-style straight below her ears, and Serena, half her age, flow and overflow, hair, clothes, talk.

They talked as if I wasn't there or as if they didn't care if I heard or as if just the opposite, they wanted me to hear.

Serena said, 'I do think it is extremely important that every single one of us gets a chance to speak when we have the Rape Talk.' Jenny agreed but she wanted to freeze the Rape Talk until they'd finished making the curtains so their safe house would be absolutely safe.

This was the scoop. They were fixing up a wreck to hide runaway wives. Like the underground railway for southern blacks who came north in the slave age. Serena and Jenny were into National Women's Aid, a programme to give women a voice. They were speaking about the refuge at a sixth-form college the following Thursday evening so they wouldn't be coming to my class.

Week five. There was a note from Lawless clipped to the outside of the register. He had officially withdrawn for personal reasons. No other notes and no one at all appeared. I don't know what got into me. I'd been there for over an hour when I looked at the register and saw the row of attendance numbers with its regular decent week-by-week from eight to two. Zero was the natural consequence. A row of zeros, a zero with my initials beside it and there it was. Done. But, as if an invisible other took over, I wrote a row of Xs and put the number eight for the number present.

Then, as if to exonerate myself, I wrote in my Little Book to Be. Evening class number five. The fiction-making gets going. Waiting for time to pass as the hands on the wall clock click and the cooling radiators cluck, our pathetic? lonely? self-serving? possibly uneasy? hero? anti-hero? sits alone on a metal chair in an empty circle. It is a dark hour, an hour fallen like light out of the moon, fallen like a heart out of the sky. Outside there is an old-fashioned English fog. It is foggy and damp with the kind of foggy damp that permeates the marrow. It feels existentially cold. The young writer-teacher pulls on his fleece-lined denim and zips it up to the collar. He turns his collar up. He sees his reflection in the window and doesn't recognize himself or the eye in the eyehole. Something in him clicks. Who would know if he left a little early? Is there anyone else in the building? Is anyone else within viewing range? He doesn't think about a BB gun. Or a book burning. He doesn't let his mind roam back to the British at war. It's a liberal era, a government under Labour. Under Jim Callaghan. He believes he has the licence to apply common sense to the circumstances. He picks up the register to return it to the shelf by the outer door and, feeling a charge like an electric current rush through him at the thought of getting out of there, he bolts for the exit.

My people, this will test your faith in human events. He was about to step into the night when the Writer walked straight into him as if he wasn't there or because he was. Let me take this from the top again. Enter the Writer carrying a heavy canvas shoulder bag, a red motorcycle helmet and a battered suitcase. He is a tall weedy thing with ears that stick out like the ears of a dormouse and as red as his scarf.

The next thing I knew I was back in the classroom backed onto one of the school desks, sitting on it, and he was unloading the contents of his suitcase onto my lap as if to anchor me or to bury me in paper. He wrote in a tiny hand in a nearly invisible pencil and had covered every sheet on both sides. He wrote between the spaces too, like Jane Austen, turning the page upside down. His sheets avalanched to the floor. This reminded him of the trauma that drove him to create. He told me about it in detail: how the sound from the bomb which hit the Roman ruin at Hobbles Lookout left him shell-shocked. At the time he was five years old. 'You remember that bomb?' he asked me as if I might have been his playmate, as if I might have grown up on his side of the Atlantic, as if I could be that old.

I wanted to go, but how could I leave? Here was a writer handing me all the material I could use in a lifetime: poems, stories, diaries, essays, radio plays. He himself was the material and his life task was its transformation. I looked at him. The guy was a wreck, a genuine destroyed package; all he could do was sputter, shuffle and write. I don't know why I didn't come right out with it and lay it on the line. Why couldn't I tell him: 'Writing is a kind of suicide. It's what you do instead of living'? His solitude was so palpable I felt it icy against my own skin. On the other hand, what is life for a writer without writing? And what about rebirth? And what about the job I had been appointed to carry out? Just for a moment I slipped inside the skin of a midwife. 'How come you're so late?' I scolded. 'This is the fifth week. It's nine o'clock and the class ends at nine.'

But he couldn't hear me. The voice inside his head was too loud.

'Now this novel,' he said, 'is called *The Red Devil*.' He put his emptied suitcase on the floor. He put his emptied bag on the floor. He put his emptied motorcycle helmet on the floor. He took his coat off, extended his long left arm, pushed up his sweater sleeve and pushed up the sleeve of his long winter underwear. 'I want you to look at my elbow,' he said, raising it to my face. 'Do you see the Red Devil?'

I couldn't see anything, but it didn't matter. The writer attached himself to me like the devil and didn't stop talking until the night was worn out and we were walking the streets of Glasgow.

You don't have to believe this. The story could go on without ending. But when I came in today, I saw the end.

Stapled to my register was a letter from Deputy Harry Noble. He wrote that there appeared to be a discrepancy between the numbers marked present for week five and the actual numbers present. Owing to this unfortunate circumstance, he was obliged to terminate my contract and would not be able to offer me employment in the future.

He concluded in these words:

We are grateful for services rendered. A payment reference slip to be submitted to the tax office is enclosed. A cheque for monies owed will be sent to your home address. Please check that the address we have for you printed below is correct in all details. May I extend our best wishes for your future endeavours?

Sincerely yours, H. Noble, Cert. Ed.

And to you, my people, sincerely yours, your writing kid,

Joey

II

October 18, 1974

Dear People,

Welcome to England's Second City. It's Birmingham as in Birmingham, Alabama; Birmingham, Michigan; Birmingham, Iowa; and Birmingham, Ohio. You spell it the same way but this is how you say it. Change 'ham' to 'hem' and drop it before it sounds. So it comes out Birming'm.

Before Christmas I had a call from the Art College in Birming'm asking if I'd like to try a day. It was a pretty good deal, thirty pounds plus expenses. That's about fifty dollars. Okay, not a fortune but a notch up on adult ed and a lot better than door-to-door market research. And let's not forget, I need to get these professional experiences under my belt.

We fixed it for the second Friday in January, short on light in any year and, as it turned out, dark to the end with sleet, hail, rain, the east wind and a humdinger of a headache. The headache came with shooting stars and bouts of retching. That got me out of bed at four a.m. and kept me up so I set off before dawn and was in Birming'm station with hours to kill. So I sat down and read the city map.

Fat help that was. The moment I set off, I was lost. Building on all sides. Sandpit after sandpit with tunnels, bridges, walls: walls coming down, walls going up; plywood, plasterboard, brick, tin, plastic, anything that could stand. Some were left bare, some partially stripped, showing layers of old wallpaper. Some were sprayed and graffitied. Just below the station, I descended into a roofed-over walkway. This was lighted with strips of hanging bulbs that looked like Christmas tree leftovers. They were blinking and winking in red and blue and white.

Builders gave me directions to the wrong college. Grateful to have arrived, I discovered that I hadn't. The towerblock housed a different college: food and domestic science. The one I was after wasn't all in one building but tucked in here and there, scattered across the city.

I never found the main building, if there was one, nor anything resembling a warehouse or workhouses for painters and sculptors, or photography labs. Eventually, however, I reached the address Phil had given me. The annexe was an old family house in a terraced row of old family houses. Extended upward, it stood tall and narrow, an old stork among its neighbours. It looked empty and when I arrived it was empty with the feeling of someone having been and gone. The wooden stairs and landing were clean-swept and gave off the sharp perfumed scent of floor-cleaning powder. In the first-floor entry room I found a table with a sign above it: UNDER NO CIRCUMSTANCE ANY BAGS OR THINGS PLACED HERE. There was a propped slate board with information in fluorescent yellow about the day's programme. Beneath my name was a list of student groups advised to attend my classes and a timetable for them that, starting at ten, ran throughout the day.

I backed into the opposite wall and let it support me. I stood there long enough to forget where I was or what I was doing and to be startled when the first student put in an appearance. Ignoring the sign forbidding use, she dropped her carpetbag on the table and shook her arm to ease it from cramp or draw my attention to the jewellery she was wearing. These were her creations made of glass and plastic and other new materials because she was a second-year student on the degree pathway in Glass, Plastics and Other New Materials. The student groups I was to teach were identified by acronyms, FADs, FASs 3Ds and so on. To help me recognize her pathway, she put her finger on the letters and spelled it out: G-P-O-N-M.

'Ga-po-num like wampum?' I tried. 'That means money in American Indian.'

She glanced at me and said nothing. I haven't a clue what she was thinking. I was thinking that she was wearing enough gaponum to win herself an Indian warrior like Hiawatha. She had gaponum on her fingers, wrists and arms, gaponum hanging round her neck, woven through her hair and needled earlobes. Her gaponum was strung on threads of leather, secured with wire and rich with beads. Stars hung from her ears. So did triangles and silver cocktail forks. As for her hair, she'd fashioned it African-style into countless braids and threaded through countless beads made to gleam. Her face was freckled and the

freckles, too, seemed to gleam. I was admiring this pheno-
menon when, unbelievably, she smiled and sang out,
'Cockles and dangles for sale for sale oh.'

Okay, so I have a heart that easily attaches and I fall for
things I imagine could exist. She was a redhead with
Anglo-Irish blood in her; and came from a town or city in
the Midlands or the North, from Merseyside or Lanca-
shire or maybe even Scarborough, but I thought of her as
my Minnehaha: Jewellery Store. An Indian maiden in
beaded boots, she had slid to my side and stood over me
watching out for my wants and needs as if brought into
this world to stand and serve.

One minute we were alone in the silent creaking
building. Then suddenly thunder on the stairs and students
thronging in. They came heavily loaded with heavy bags
and in heavy dead men's coats – Salvation Army store
giveaways – and wearing workmen's boots. They closed in
to release their bags onto a heap, making a mountain on
the forbidden table. My name began to circulate. Who was
I? Where was I? Was I going to show?

What I wanted to know was: where was the classroom?
And where was Phil Goodacre? He was the one who'd
phoned me and I'd assumed he'd be there to tell me what
to do. Jewellery Store said that she didn't think Phil was
coming in because they were having Creative Writing with
Mr Schechter. She pronounced it 'Sha-hec'ta'.

'Schechter,' I said, giving it a German sound, giving myself
away and so taking on the responsibility I didn't feel up to.

She tipped her head as if to study me from a different
perspective. 'Hang on a sec. Are you?' I nodded. 'So you're
a writer, then. And you've got to teach us?'

'Yup,' I said. 'Looks like I'm prof for the day.'

'Oh you poor thing,' she burst out as if I'd just walked
headfirst into a glass door.

'We'll see how it goes,' I said, hoping I was hiding my true feelings.

By now the crowd was beginning to turn away. In another moment they'd be out the door and I'd be out of students. 'Hi hi,' I used my loud voice, 'I'm Joey Schechter. I'm here to take the class. But you're going to have to tell me where to take it.'

They told me and took me. The place was on the other side of the terrace past a sex shop advertising itself in a giant stiletto shoe and so veiled in dust I took it for bankrupt and abandoned. But it wasn't. It was business as usual inside. The dust came from the digging that was going on all over the city.

On the way they explained how things worked in Phil's department. Things were kind of free or creative. Sometimes Phil gave them the day off. Sometimes they had a guest lecture in the Great Hall. Or he arranged something special like me, Creative Writing. If he said he was coming in, he'd be there. The problem was Spaghetti Junction. Motorway snarl-up. One birdbrain does one daft thing and that's it. You're stuck.

Builder's dust veiled the Grills Onion and Sausage Café and inside there was smoke and steam. The coffee was deplorable but the place was okay. Half a dozen booths and no other customers. In no time, the students had squeezed themselves in and set themselves up with paper and pens, rolling papers and tobacco, fruit suckers and, to account for all tastes and diets, carrots, celery and black radishes.

I had prepared, overprepared, to tell the truth. I'd been jotting down topics for days and I'd carefully copied them into a list and I'd remembered to bring it. In the confusion of the moment, however, I forgot everything. All I could think was: I'm here. Where was here?

I looked around. I said, 'Look around.' What did I see?
I asked them, 'What do you see?' The walls were mustard
yellow, the edging in art deco gilt and purple. I breathed
for smell. I could smell bitter Nescafé, burnt toast, refried
lard and bacon. 'What do you smell?' I closed my eyes.
'Close your eyes,' I said. 'What do you hear?' I heard a
phone ringing. It rang and it went on ringing. It was still
ringing when I opened my eyes to look for it. Where was
the sound coming from? It was coming down from the
ceiling from a swing hanging beside the fluorescent light.
Or rather from a green bird perched on the swing beside
the light.

'Oh my God,' I said.

'That's not God. That's our baby,' the students informed
me. 'That's Lulu. We're giving him lessons. One of these
days, it'll get through his little bird brain and he'll stop
ringing to answer.'

That was enough. I had my trigger words. 'Write these
down,' I said. 'Baby. Telephone. Parrot. Paris. Take sixty
seconds, then start writing whatever comes to mind. Don't
think. Just write.'

My people, it worked. No Tittensors and Proudloves
burdened with babies and battered wives. No Lawlesses
with a marriage crisis in Bradford. No apologies and ex-
planations about why not. These were art students. Three
or four questions and, with a humming buzz, they were
off. Bodies leaned this way and that. Smoke, steam, and
warmth radiated. Food was cooking. A telephone rang
and rang. A parrot speaking in his way. I could see a future
for myself being a prof like this.

For quarter of an hour I sat there looking on and thinking. When they were ready we'd have a read around, hear
what they'd done, applaud and then talk about rewrites.
To make the work better and better and better. Meanwhile

I could dream, and for a few minutes I did, resting where I sat among them, only gradually aware of Jewellery Store gradually pressing closer. When she stood up I woke with a start. 'What's the matter?'

'Time to go back.'

'But we just got here.'

'Phil will be waiting.'

How did she know? I looked from her to the other students. As if on cue they were all packing up to leave.

So back we went past the building site, past the dusty sex shop and up the sunken wooden stairs to Phil's office.

This time the door was open and Phil was standing in the doorway. He was tall and he was wearing a long tweed coat with a bright red scarf. He was deep in conversation with someone who looked familiar.

I suppose I shouldn't have been surprised. How large is England after all? The size of the state of Texas, or of the New England states? And how large is the West Midlands? How large Greater Birming'm? Really, it was quite reasonable: a woman interested in creative writing is a likely candidate for a degree in Fine Art.

By now you've probably guessed it was Serena, Serena from Hobbles End, the bright spark Serena who recommended *Fear of Flying* with its zipless fuck which led to the book burning by Eleanor Tittensor and the termination of my teaching contract with that authority. Serena Bronx-Henchy, mother of three or four, spokesperson for battered wives who, before she fell pregnant by Henchy, a 'bricky' – bricklayer, I knew this much – had been headed for medical school.

To find her standing in Phil's office caught me by surprise. I stopped still, staring with Jewellery Store at my side.

Where do I draw the line between knowing and suspecting, between public and private, between the things of the world and the temptations of the heart? I'll tell you this much. Phil looked old enough to be Serena's father and he looked uncomfortably warm. When he took off his coat he revealed how immaculately a man could dress: black pinstripe three-piece suit with a gold chain that looped between the pockets of his waistcoat as if to keep him in his clothes. Above this, shaved and scented, a face: craggy, gentle, compelling. Serena kept looking at him as they kept talking and he kept looking at Serena. She was wearing the clothes I remembered, long skirt, blouse with blossoming sleeve, a long silk scarf and several long necklaces. Her glossy hair hung long and loose.

With a sudden shiver that sounded a ding of metal against glass, Jewellery Store broke it up. The two of them looked up and noticed us.

As they say in the movies, 'Action stations.'

Phil, who had come in to sort me out, put his coat back on. He had me sign my pay claim form, gave me a set of keys with instructions about where to hide them and ex-plained that he would not be back until Monday. He had some business in London by which he meant a funeral to attend.

Under the circumstances, his office was mine for the day. Suddenly we were a world away from the Grills Onion and Sausage Café; in book heaven, or hell. Phil's office was a high-ceilinged chamber with tall windows and in-built shelves, where books were double-packed and squeezed in and stacked high all around. There was a boardroom table with a dozen chairs. The chairs, too, were stacked with books: the history of civilization, art, literature, science, the philosophies of East and West. I was ready to read titles for the next six hours.

But the students, Serena among them, weren't bothered by the books. They got down to work. Like experienced campers, they made themselves space where they could. Chairs pushed out of the way, they sat under and around the table in inventive positions: in yoga folds and stretched out on their sides or bellies propped on an elbow – one hand for the chin, the other for the pen. When there was no more floor space, which happened before lunch as students kept arriving and no one left, they stood against the wall. Pressing their notepads to the spines of books, they wrote standing up. Those who needed help because the words wouldn't flow turned to those who couldn't stop the flow and everyone turned in something. Those who preferred drawing offered cartoons with bubble-speech, telling stories around images of baby, parrot, telephone and Parisian berets.

'We encourage them to apply creative thinking to all aspects of the world we live in,' the Future Studies guy explained to me at lunch. 'We have some quite able students. Look at Louise Kelly. Is that a woman or a walking market stall? Every time I see her she is waltzing around in a new collection.'

So that was Jewellery Store. Not much of a creative writer but it looked like she might be an ace at marketing.

We spent the afternoon together – strange, quiet, companionable – just the two of us because after lunch, save for Jewellery Store, the students disappeared. Wherever they went, it looked as if they took the afternoon group with them because no one else showed up. Jewellery Store and I cleared two chairs and some table space. By then I had a weight of their creative work to get through and so I started reading. When I came to Serena's or as soon as I was in it, I must admit, a groan escaped me. The words at her command! And what she did with them. The wit! The music! The resonance! After the groan, a gasp. I'd more than met my match. I'd met my mistress. But later, later for that.

Taking breaks, I browsed through Phil's books, wanting to borrow most of them. I settled on one, planning to return it when I came back to talk about how things stood job-wise. All afternoon, maintaining a nunlike silence and using book stacks as separators, Jewellery Store sorted and rearranged beads. The finale took place at five p.m. As I was gathering my things, I sent books and beads flying. Collecting the books was one thing but the beads had dug into the carpet like ticks into cat's fur. They had us on our hands and knees and then our bellies. Some time along the way I collected a few sliver cuts. I didn't notice until I was on the train looking at Phil's book and saw my bloodstains on the page.

That was enough of that. What a day. My headache. The weather. The early train. The crazy maze of a city. Then Jewellery Store. As if that wasn't enough, Serena. And all those students writing and then vanishing. And Rob Sutter who came in specially to show me where to go for lunch and which beer to order. There's home-brew and home-brew and he was expert. What more? He was my age with a wife, two kids and a published novel and he runs marathons. To keep fit he's out every morning before breakfast running through Black Heath, wherever that is, and around the university park. About the way Phil was dressed, Rob said, it was the Romantic in him. Phil puts on a white shirt to sit at his desk at home and today it was a Highgate funeral. In the cemetery where Karl Marx is buried. For a five-year-old. The child died like Socrates of hemlock poisoning. On holiday with her grandparents in Ireland. Just like that. Phil likes to attend ceremonies and he likes to go to London and make the rounds of the bookshops.

When I reached London, I saw Phil crossing Euston Station to catch his train back to Birming'm. He'd bought as many 'finds' as he could carry and he was lugging them in bulging carrier bags. Seeing me, he said, 'Just the man I was looking for.' He put his bags down to fish something out. 'I found the book,' he said.

I didn't know what he was on about. 'The book?'

'The book with your letters in it.'

'My letters?'

He handed me a thin soft-covered book and, picking up his bags, excused himself. 'Gotta go. We'll talk soon.' And he was gone.

The book was a set of unpublished proofs. In it were two of my letters to you people under the title 'An Ace in the Midlands'. Explain this one to me. It brought my headache back with a vengeance like a spear between the eyes and a twist of knots in the neck. I felt as if I was going to start retching. As I pushed myself towards the men's room at the opposite end of the station, the lights broke into threads and beads and started spinning. It was no laughing matter. When I had recovered enough to look at the pages I recognized my own words. But they were old words. They were the wrong words. It was the wrong draft. These letters should have gone into Eleanor Tittensor's fire instead of Erica Jong's satire on the Wife of Bath's tale.

That night I felt pretty awful, but in the morning I put on a clean shirt, took a stroll past Keats's House and onto Hampstead Heath over to Highgate where Coleridge bought his laudanum and thought I could try again. Maybe I could do it better.

About the Editor

PAUL MCDONALD is Senior Lecturer in English at the University of Wolverhampton. His published work includes books on the fiction of the industrial Midlands, and the American writer Philip Roth. His first novel, *Surviving Sting*, was heralded as 'a voice from the Black Country as authentic as baltis and Banks's bitter' (*Time Out*). Paul lives in Walsall where, to his horror, he finds he's developing a taste for chunky jewellery and combat dogs.